# The Torment
# of Sherlock Holmes

# The Torment
# of Sherlock Holmes

## Val Andrews

**BREESE
BOOKS
LONDON**

First published in 2000 by
Breese Books Ltd
164 Kensington Park Road, London W11 2ER, England

© Breese Books Ltd, 2000

ISBN: 0 947533 23 0

Front cover photograph
is reproduced by kind permission of
Retrograph Archive, London

Typeset in 11½/14pt Caslon by
Ann Buchan (Typesetters), Middlesex
Printed and bound in the United States of America

# CHAPTER 1

# The Tormented Detective

The strange events which I am about to relate took place in the spring of the year 1897. Earlier that year my friend Mr Sherlock Holmes had begun to suffer from an illness brought upon him through overwork, lack of restful sleep, exposure to the elements and, although I hate to admit it, his addictions to certain substances. (Addictions, by the way, which he had always denied, claiming that his use of cocaine, for example, was simply to bring a little excitement into the duller stages of his existence.) Dr Moore Agar of Harley Street had been consulted and had warned my friend that only changes of scene and regime could ward off a complete breakdown of the kind that could easily end his distinguished career. Holmes reluctantly agreed to take a vacation. However, as my readers will know, this interlude had plunged Holmes, by chance, straight back into active investigative activity. Seemingly recovered, he had insisted upon returning to Baker Street where he had immersed himself in his professional work, causing Dr Moore Agar to wash his hands of the matter.

Of course, inevitably, the predicted complete breakdown had occurred but more quickly and with even more severity than even I had feared. It produced first fits of depression and irritability, sleeplessness and loss of appetite. Yet worse still was to follow with the world's only consulting detective retreating for the most part into a world of his own.

Dear reader, please believe me when I say that I did whatever I could to help my poor friend, risking his anger in my efforts to get him to eat, sleep, or even to communicate. He had once referred to me as his closest, nay, his only friend, yet in his distress he was proved wrong for Mrs Hudson and young Billy were more than just concerned, as was Inspector Lestrade. Yes, George Lestrade was a frequent seeker after information concerning Holmes's condition. But sadly these were just honest, kindly and direct people with little real understanding of the nature of his malady.

As can be imagined, the large number of potential clients seeking Holmes's assistance had to be informed that he was seriously unwell and dealing with them became so difficult and time-consuming for me that I was forced eventually to enlist the aid of the press. Needless to say, I did not convey to journalists the true nature of his illness.

Sherlock's brother, Mycroft Holmes, was a tower of strength, prising himself from his armchair at the Diogenes Club to visit his ailing brother frequently. He would sit by the hour beside the lacklustre detective, though never making the mistake of seeming to press him to converse, yet giving him the opportunity to do so. Mycroft frequently pressed large sums of money upon both Mrs Hudson and myself, knowing as he did that Sherlock's financial affairs could not be dealt with until there was some improvement in my friend's health.

He would say: 'My dear Watson, I know you will do what you can for him, regardless of cost. He respects and trusts you more than any other being and if it is God's will that he should recover his strength and interest in life, I feel sure that you will be the first to know of it.'

Mycroft's concern for his younger brother was touching, especially for me. I had always respected the man and admired his talents which had made it possible for him to 'sometimes *be* the British Government' and all from a padded chair in a London club from which through the years I had seldom seen him move before this crisis. To see him heave his elegant bulk so frequently up the stairs of 221B Baker Street was something which I would not have predicted.

One Monday morning, when Holmes's condition had remained unaltered for weeks rather than days, I had arisen at a late hour to find my friend already seated at the breakfast table, doing little more than play with his food. Oh how I longed for him to chastise me as of yore with some biting remark concerning my tardiness in rising. I noted that the newspapers were still pristine from Mrs Hudson's iron. Holmes nodded curtly and muttered something which, with a great stretch of the imagination, might have been taken for a 'Good morning'. As I poured coffee and ladled kedgeree a look of utter disgust crossed my friend's lean and tortured face. He arose from the table and tottered to his chair by the fireplace. There he sat, head down, for all the world like a heap of bones wrapped in a faded crimson dressing gown.

Guiltily, and without any kind of joy in it, I managed a little breakfast, eventually rising to place *The Thunderer* upon the arm of his chair. I nudged the long-neglected clay pipe so that it was within his reach and glanced insinuatingly at the Turkish slipper. Then, opening one of the other newspapers, I sat in the chair opposite to that of my friend.

The eyes of Sherlock Holmes glowed like two hot coals, seeming to be the only life he presented. Those eyes spoke to me and said, 'Watson, if I wish to smoke or read I will do so. But at this moment I wish to do neither, and desire no company save my own.' I could only wish that he had actually spoken the words, however discouraging, but I took the hint and, donning my greatcoat, I left the rooms for a stroll in Regent's Park.

I watched the squirrels without my usual interest in their scamperings as I strode without enthusiasm along the Broadwalk in the direction of the zoological gardens. I tried to clear my mind but could not cast aside the welfare of my friend from it. Would Sherlock Holmes never again be able to use his great gifts for the good of humanity in general and needful individuals in particular; and would there be no more exploits for me to chronicle, the game never more to be afoot? This being so, I must inevitably return to being just an ordinary medical practitioner without that excitement provided by the best and wisest man I had ever known. I recalled how dull my life had been during that time when Holmes had been absent from the scene and presumed dead. Some three years earlier he had reappeared like a phoenix from the ashes to enliven my life once more. Now I felt that I must resign myself to the loss of my friend's participation in my life, and possibly (although I tried to cast the thought aside) even the loss of my dear friend altogether; for as a medical man I had to confess my fear not simply for his mind but for his very life itself.

Thus sadly preoccupied I took very little notice of my fellow perambulators, until one individual stood out to the extent of attracting even my preoccupied attention. A black-clad and heavily veiled woman of striking and shapely figure caught my eye. I remember thinking that she must have been recently widowed which was sad and rare in such a young woman (for she gave a youthful impression in spite of her veil).

She walked briskly and, as we passed each other, she dropped what appeared to be a small scrap of paper. I bent to retrieve it wishing to assure myself that it was no more than a discarded omnibus ticket before interrupting her reverie. However, it proved to be a receipt for an item of luggage lodged at Victoria Station. I turned to pursue the lady in order to return it, only to find that she had moved surprisingly quickly and was lost in a crowd of people. I spent five or six minutes trying to trace her without success before I seated myself upon a park bench to consider my next stop.

I studied the ticket, attempting by habit to apply those

methods which long association with Sherlock Holmes had made habitual. But there was little to be deduced from it, there being merely the usual printed matter and number on its face and some small print on the reverse setting forth the terms under which luggage could be lodged. The correct and obvious thing to do was to hand in the ticket, either at a police station, lost property office, or at Victoria Station itself.

There was, I knew, a lost property office at Baker Street Station and I started to stride in the direction of that place as manfully as my game leg would allow, in order to end my own involvement with the veiled lady and her left luggage ticket. Yet, as I neared my goal, a sudden rather daring and, by my own standards, a rather shady thought entered my mind . . .

Suppose instead I were to journey to Victoria, claim the item and take it back to 221B Baker Street, in the vague hope that Sherlock Holmes might be tempted to interest himself in the minor mystery of tracing its owner? If my scheme failed I could, I told myself, easily return the item with some invention concerning having claimed it in error. If it aroused my friend to the extent that he, once again took some interest in life around him, then surely my minor deception would be justified? Of course, I lived in the hope of finding my friend improved making my wild scheme unnecessary, nonetheless the ticket was still in my waistcoat pocket when I opened the door of 221B.

As I entered the house I was waylaid by an anxious Mrs Hudson. The poor woman wrung her hands and said, 'Doctor, I must speak with you about Mr Holmes.'

I said, 'Of course, Mrs Hudson, please speak freely!'

She cast her eyes downward as she said, 'Since he has been unwell he has kept himself to himself, as one might say. But, Doctor, when I took him a cup of coffee at noon he ignored me completely and just stared into space like a body in a trance. Try as I might, short of showing complete disrespect, I could not get him to answer me or even seem to realize that I was there.' (The poor dear soul began to weep.) 'Oh, Dr Watson, what are we going to do? His mind has always been as sharp as a razor, but I fear for it, and I fear for him . . .'

I comforted the poor faithful lady as best I could, then hastened up the stairs to judge my friend's condition for myself.

There he sat, just as Mrs Hudson had described him, with his body slumped in his chair, his head bowed, yet with his eyes upturned and staring straight before him. I decided to make light of it, as if his condition were quite normal, saying, 'It's a blustery day, Holmes, even for the time of year. I had a good walk though.'

At this point, having perceived no reaction from my friend, I threw caution to the winds and casting all subtlety aside I increased the volume of my voice and said, 'In the park I saw a rather strange veiled woman in widow's weeds. She dropped a cloakroom ticket which I managed to retrieve.'

At this point I realized that even a minor explosion would be unlikely to attract his attention. I feared what I had for some time suspected was true and that my friend was extremely ill indeed. An eminent specialist having refused to treat him further, how could I, a simple general practitioner, help my poor dear friend?

Casting all ethics aside and, grasping at the only straw which presented itself, I turned the collar of his robe against the draught, placed a rug over his knees and set forth for Victoria. It was habit rather than caution which made me ignore the first two cabs to present themselves and to hail the third. The equipage pulled out of a mews, the horse aged and the driver seedy, but I clambered in and shouted 'Victoria Station', settling back, soon to be deep in thought. Those wretched ethics started to trouble me again and my mission was in the balance as we neared the busy railway.

I noticed that the driver was turning into a side street just short of the destination. As I leaned out of the hansom to remonstrate with the cabby, the vehicle slowed to a stop and to my amazement the door was pulled open and I was dragged out into the street by a ruffian, attired like some Irish navvy. In desperation I looked to the driver for support only to see the shabby vehicle disappear from my view with a surprising turn of speed. The ruffian shook me by the lapels and growled, "Ere you, 'and over that there ticket!'

Although without my service revolver, I had a stout malacca in my grasp. Thrusting him from me I followed this advantage up by bringing the cane down sharply upon his shoulder. This action seemed to dismay him and distract from his purpose. Then, as I made a threatening gesture as if to deliver more blows with the cane, he hastily retreated and, turning a corner, disappeared from my gaze.

I was only slightly shaken by this experience and furthermore it only had the effect of dispelling those doubts which had been clouding my mind. Someone, I realized, wanted that luggage receipt to the extent of taking a great deal of trouble to wrest it from me. Certainly they had used a ruffian to waylay me and very possibly had provided me with an especially arranged hansom, even if it had been the third to present itself. Bearing all this in mind I made for Victoria Station with renewed determination!

With some trepidation I presented the numbered ticket to the left luggage clerk, hoping that he would not demand any further identification. I took a quick glance at the boxes and cases on the shelves and more by luck than judgement my eyes lit upon a brown hat box bearing a number matching that of the ticket which I held.

I muttered, 'My sister asked me to pick up her Sunday bonnet. It's in a brown hat box and, by Jove, I'm dashed if I don't see it on the shelf!'

Despite my words the clerk, evidently not overburdened with intellect, looked at my ticket and searched for the number, ignoring my indications. But when he did locate it, to my consternation, he gave the hat box a lively shake which produced a sound evidently made by a hard object within. He said, 'Summick else in 'ere an' all, summick 'ard!'

But with great presence of mind I said, 'That will be her lorgnette. The poor old thing is blind as a bat without them.'

This time, following my recent experience, I simply took the first cab to present itself, though taking the precaution of noting down the driver's number before clambering in with my hat box. I could tell from his righteous indignation that he was an honest fellow, a belief reflected in the shilling over and above the fare which I paid him when we reached Baker Street.

In the sitting room of 221B I found Holmes sitting, lost in his crimson robe, exactly as I had left him an hour or so before. I would have been willing to swear from his appearance that he had not moved as much as an eyelid, let alone a muscle. I dropped the hat box heavily onto the floor, causing that object to rattle once more.

I detected no sign from my friend that he had even been aware of this action so I decided to proceed, using my own poor imitation of his methods, speaking my thoughts aloud. First, I narrated a version of my adventure with the ruffian, the seedy hansom and my reclamation of the hat box. Then I continued, 'So what have we here, a large brown hat box, obviously originally the property of a lady of means, for its quality is considerable despite its worn appearance. The box has, not unnaturally, been closed and secured by a woman, in view of the neatness with which the tapes have been tied . . .'

I pulled upon the ribbons to untie them, allowing me to lift the top half of the box clear and at the same time to take a sly squint at my poor friend, which revealed to me no flicker of reaction.

Manfully I carried on. 'What have we here? Not a hat as might be expected, but what appears to be a rather costly ladies' gown.'

Lifting out the garment, so much creased through being

crammed into the hat box, I held it up to the light that I might examine it more fully. It was cream coloured, heavy silk with black fur trimmings. A reddish stain spanned the area between the centre of the neckline and the waistband and just below the neckline there was a slit, as if made by a knife or dagger.

I continued with my little drama. 'Costly, but badly stained from breast to waist with what appears to be blood, its point of origin seeming to be a rip made by a blade!'

Deeper in the box, beneath some bloodstained under-garments, I discovered that which had rattled; it appeared to be some kind of carving knife. My voice must have shaken as I continued, 'What have we here? If I am not mistaken, the instrument of cause for the slit and bloodstains . . . a carving knife!'

So saying, I shot another furtive glance at Holmes and to my great satisfaction I realized that my histrionics had gained some sort of reaction. He had raised his head so that his great beak of a nose seemed to be directed toward the knife which I held. His eyes no longer stared aimlessly before him but had become like gimlets as of yore. I scarcely dared to breathe, and at long last he spoke. 'It is a butcher's knife!'

Very faint, yet distinct was his voice, prompting me to ask, trying to conceal my excitement, 'What did you say, Holmes?'

'I said, Watson, that it is a butcher's knife rather than a mere carver. There is a difference you know.'

He extended a claw-like hand to take the knife as his other hand searched for his lens through which he peered at the blade and hilt. Then he rose, albeit unsteadily and tottered rather than walked to his bench, where he began to potter with his microscope, saying, 'Analysis seems hardly necessary, my dear Watson, for with such evidence the blood must surely be human; yet in my profession I long ago learned that one can take nothing for granted.' He paused as he passed a hand across his brow. 'I fear that I am somewhat weak, Watson, but some of Mrs Hudson's excellent beef broth will soon put that right.'

When that good lady carried in the tray bearing a steaming bowl and a piece of bread, she did so with a triumphant air. She placed the tray upon the table. 'Mr Holmes, I am so glad to see that you are feeling a little better. I will prepare a light supper for you, perhaps a scrambled egg . . .' Her voice trailed off as the tears came to the eyes of the dear faithful lady.

But as for Holmes, he made light of it all, although the change in him after some broth and a little bread was hard to believe. 'I have been foolish, Watson, selfish and foolish, allowing my own depression to torment those nearest to me. I apologize and I will see that it does not happen again.'

There was warmth in my heart for the first time in weeks. 'Holmes, my dear fellow, this sudden improvement in your spirit fills me with joy and no sort of apology is needed.'

The bizarre widow who had dropped that luggage ticket had my gratitude at that moment, whatever part she might have played in the tragedy which the contents of the hat box seemed to indicate. Sherlock Holmes filled a clay pipe with dark shag and lit it with a vesta. I had never thought that the acrid fumes he produced would be as welcome to me as if they had been attar of violets! Indeed, the strong narcotic seemed almost to complete a recovery which the broth had begun. The colour was starting to creep back into his ashen face.

In a little while he turned his attention again to the chemistry bench and when he spoke to me again his voice was all but restored to its normal cadence. 'It is as we supposed, Watson, human blood on both the dress and the blade of the butcher's knife, and of the same kind save for some traces of the bovine kind near the hilt as one might expect from such an instrument of trade. The hat box originated in Paris and the dress was fashioned at about the time of that affair at Baskerville Hall. I am no expert on ladies' fashions, Watson, but I am observant enough to have noticed that these great leg-of-mutton sleeves have been out of favour for some years. So it is an expensive gown so worn by a well-to-do lady unmindful of the latest fads.'

'But, Holmes, could the outmoded style not denote that we are looking at what remains of some long passed tragedy?'

'No, the blood is recent, yet there remains the possibility that the victim was wearing a dress other than her own. For example, a maid wearing a dress passed on to her by her mistress. But one thing is beyond doubt, we are looking at the evidence of a recent tragedy which must have resulted in the death or at least grave injury of the wearer of this garment.'

His quick fingers searched the recesses of the box for further evidence and eventually his right hand emerged clutching a small scrap of paper. 'Where there is lining paper, Watson, always search beneath it for some trifle that might have been overlooked.' He held up the scrap of paper like a conjurer holds up a playing card and asked, 'Am I right?'

The paper which was of poor quality was about an inch wide and some two-and-a-half inches long, serrated upon both short edges. Obviously it had been torn from a ticket roll and bore the message 'Dolphin's Span. One Half Penny'.

I said, 'Obviously a ticket given for the payment of a halfpenny, in return for being conveyed by some form of public transport. It is not a ticket for a railway journey for if so it would bear more details and almost certainly cost more than half a penny. Perhaps a ticket to ride some country bus?'

'My dear Watson, you amaze me and it is so refreshing to hear again some of your inaccurate deductions! A country omnibus, perhaps pulled by a single horse? How idyllic, but no, I feel that the word "Dolphin" denotes a maritime connection. "Span" would suggest a bridge so I deduce that we have a ticket to cross over a toll bridge of some kind. The involvement of Victoria Station might narrow a coastal search to that of southern England, perhaps between Dover and Littlehampton. Be so good, Watson, as to pass me the atlas of the south of England.'

I admit to having felt a little put out through his dismissals of my deductions, as put out as one can be with a dear friend miraculously restored from what had seemed to be a permanent state of uninterest in all about him. 'There must be hundreds of rivers with toll bridges shown in your atlas . . .'

'Yes, but not titled "Dolphin Span", Watson. Ah, here it is; there is just such a titled bridge spanning the River Arun, near Rustington, a little south of Arundel. There is a large sandbank, or small island, named Dolphin Spine. Please pass me my album covered in pink paper with the large inkstain upon it, old fellow, if you would be so good.'

Sherlock Holmes recharged his pipe and settled again in the armchair, having first surrounded it with maps, albums and scrapbooks. He was not as yet perhaps quite the Holmes of old, yet in comparison with that sad creature that I had encountered upon my return from Regent's Park, a veritable dynamo! He searched his ephemera, I assumed, for anything relating to Dolphin Spine, south of Arundel. It now became obvious to me that he intended to pursue this matter of the unknown woman evidently stabbed to death. Under more normal circumstances I would have questioned the advisability of his involvement in a matter which he had not been invited to investigate. I might even have dared to suggest that we hand all our findings to the police, but the circumstances were not normal. My ruse to interest him in that which I had expected to be a trivial matter had worked beyond my expectations and not for the first time that day I cast aside all my sense of ethics. Any illegality would be my own and I was willing to serve a prison sentence rather than allow my friend to sink back into a mental abyss.

Having found at least some of the information that he was seeking, Holmes told me that Dolphin Spine was known locally as Shack Island, on account of the shed-like bungalows erected upon it in recent years to house holiday-makers as well as artists and writers of a reclusive nature.

'We must journey to the south coast without delay, Watson.'

I started, thinking he meant at once, but it was soon clear that even Holmes realized the folly of such an action. 'I mean after a hot meal, a good night's sleep and an early breakfast. Then I will be ready for anything. I assume, Watson, that you are willing to accompany me, if your own plans will permit?'

'I have nothing, Holmes, that I cannot defer.' What I did not add was, 'If you think I am going to allow you to make a journey on your own in your present state of health, you are much mistaken.'

Holmes lingered at the dinner table and between courses he explained to me that he was feeling stronger with every passing minute. He retired early, his short return to normality having tired him. But I was in no hurry to turn in myself and I rang for Mrs Hudson to beg her for a final pot of coffee.

When she entered the room with it she, too, had been transformed, her face wreathed in a happy smile. 'Doctor, you really are a marvel and no mistake, sir. I don't quite know what you did, but whatever it was it worked like a charm. Did you see how he cleared his plate? Oh, God bless you, Dr Watson, God bless you!'

Naturally I made light of my own small part in Holmes's miraculous recovery. Yet secretly I wondered with a shudder what might have happened had I not noticed that dropped cloakroom ticket or, having done so, decided that it was no concern of mine!

# CHAPTER 2

# The Dolphin's Spine

The following morning found Holmes and me speeding from Victoria to Brighton at more than fifty miles an hour. Unfortunately in our rush to catch the departing train we had been forced to occupy a non-smoking compartment. With the train being an express, there was no opportunity for us to change compartments. Naturally I restrained from smoking but Holmes simply made a compromise in lighting a Turkish cigarette instead of a pipe. I reprimanded him mildly. 'Really, Holmes, there may be no one else in the carriage, but rules are rules, you know!'

To my surprise and amazement, Holmes burst into an explosion of laughter. When I told him that I failed to see the humour of the situation, he spoke between wheezes of merriment. 'Oh, Watson, really you will be the death of me yet! First you find a cloakroom ticket and instead of handing it in to the proper authority, you illegally claim someone else's hat box. You then involve a highly respectable detective in your madcap escapade . . . and then . . . oh, my

goodness, then . . . you reprimand *him* for smoking a cigarette in a non-smoking carriage!'

Conveniently, of course, he failed to make mention of his
own enthusiasm to investigate the matter, also the whole
matter of leaving Scotland Yard out of the issue and the
episodes of the ruffian and the bogus hansom cab.

In little more than an hour we had reached Brighton,
where we were to make our connection with the westbound
train. At the bookstall Holmes purchased a number of
newspapers, local and national, prior to our piling into the
train to Bognor. This time I made sure that we found a
smoker, even if the carriage was a little crowded. There
were already seated an elderly lady who drew her voluminous coat about her in a defensive manner, a pale-faced
cleric who studied his newspaper, a respectably dressed
young man sporting a bowler hat and a middle-aged lady
with a cat basket upon the seat beside her who dabbed her
face at intervals with her handkerchief. I studied them but
briefly, and as far as I could see, Holmes not at all.

Yet as we occupied opposite corner seats at the far end,
he leaned forward to speak to me. 'Watson, purely as an
exercise, what do you make of our fellow passengers?'

He had spoken softly that only I might hear him. I shot
them each a further furtive glance before replying. 'Not a
great deal, save that the old lady in the corner is, in my
medical opinion, an asthmatic; she is very short of breath.
The clergyman seems to have found an article in his paper
to greatly interest him; probably of ecclesiastic interest. I
can make nothing notable about the man in the bowler hat,
but I notice that the other lady has a cat basket yet no cat,

for the top of the basket is open. From this and the frequent use of her 'kerchief I deduce that she mourns a much loved pet which she has just had the terrible experience of taking to be put to sleep.'

I was quite proud of my use of Holmes's methods, though hoping that I had left something of significance for him to opine, especially in view of his recent lack of mental activity. But a glance at him, allied to long experience, told me that he was far from impressed with my deductions.

'My dear fellow, I thought you understood our methods far better than to parade these inaccuracies before me. The old lady, for instance. Far from being asthmatic, she has been gasping to regain her breath having been rushing to catch her train. You will notice that she is somewhat stout, and her gasping becomes less frequent as she gradually regains her wind. She left home in a great hurry as exemplified by her purple blouse and green skirt. No lady so well established would have so little dress sense under ideal conditions. See how she clutches her greatcoat around her, having realized her mistake. The man in the bowler hat has suffered hard times but things for him have taken a turn for the better.'

Feeling that he was overplaying his cards, I said as much, but he insisted, 'Exactly, Watson, you fail to see that which is right in front of you. Notice the soaped and trimmed coat sleeve, yet his hat is brand new and he travels on a first-class ticket. He has not yet had time to make the long overdue visit to his tailor.'

I grunted and asked what he made of the vicar.

'I make of him that he is not reading the newspaper,

which you have failed to notice he holds upside down. But he is reading, therefore the newspaper is a cover for something unbecoming to his cloth. Probably a socialist tract or something of the kind.'

As if to illustrate Holmes's statement, the vicar dropped his newspaper to reveal that he was holding a political journal. His blush quite matched his politics. Yet I felt that I must have scored a hit with my views on the lady with the cat basket.

But here again Holmes destroyed my logic. 'Finally we will come to the lady with the wicker box. She has not been weeping, Watson, for her rouge and face flour remain unstreaked. No, she has a spring cold, and the open top of the basket indicates that she uses it to transport her shopping. I see a glimpse of blue sugar paper and a paper bag which doubtless contains eggs. Such a basket gives better protection for such breakables than does a shopping bag.'

As if on a theatrical cue, the lady sneezed into her handkerchief, leaving the train at Hove. At Shoreham the others descended, the old lady making a dash for the exit unsuitable for one of her years and build.

Holmes tossed me a local newspaper. 'See if you can find me any item concerning a missing woman.'

As I scanned the pages I thought of how great had been my friend's recovery in just a few short hours. He had even recovered his seeming ability to read my mind.

'Yes, Watson, I am much recovered, but were I fully restored I believe I would have gleaned even more from an observation of our fellow passengers. However, we progress, my dear fellow, we progress!'

Eventually we reached our destination, which was Rustington, and having alighted from the train and emerged from the station we glanced about us for the sight of a cab or other vehicle that might be plying for hire. Eventually we espied a rather seedy-looking four-wheeler with a rather aged horse between its shafts and a shabby man in its driving seat.

He jumped down and gave us a military salute, his mournful features attempting an ingratiating smile. 'Take you wherever you want to go, gents. Don't judge us by appearances, we goes at a spanking pace, old Captain and me!'

Rather to my amazement Holmes insisted upon examining the horse, first opening its mouth to inspect its teeth, then running a hand over its forelegs, paying particular attention to the knees. Then he looked at its hindquarters before saying, 'Did you ride him yourself in the Afghan war?'

He started. 'How did you know I was in the cavalry, guv'nor?'

'It is obvious, my dear fellow, from your stance and the cut of your whiskers. A non-commissioned officer, I imagine. As for the horse, he is about twenty years old and bears the British Army brand. I thought I might risk a calculated guess?'

He smiled broadly. 'Bless you, sir, you've almost hit the nail on the head. We were both in India at the time of the Afghan campaign, but I didn't ride him for he was a pack horse. I knew he'd been a good 'un though, but he'd had a fall you see, so was demoted from being an officer's mount to being a pack horse. You looked at his knees, so you can imagine what happened in that mountainous terrain. It was not his fault that he stumbled, but once they do they never trust them to be a charger again. Never mind, it possibly saved his life. Then after the war I heard that he was in a sale of old army horses and I bought him for a song. We've been together ever since and we manages to earn a crust, old Captain and me! Do you know this old horse saved an officer's life in the battle of Maiwand? He was my officer too, surgeon he was to be exact. He got badly shot in the shoulder, so I managed to get him up onto old Captain. Then I pointed the horse toward HQ and give him a slap and I heard afterwards that he got the surgeon safely back.'

It was my turn to try and recall that which was hazy. I had indeed been badly injured at Maiwand and had arrived back at our headquarters slumped over the back of a pack horse. After that I had been extremely ill for weeks, and have never really been able to exactly recollect what happened after I was shot.

I gasped, 'Is it Corporal Murray that stands before us?'

The cabby's turn it was to gasp. 'Doctor, Dr Watson, can it be you?'

I grasped him by the shoulders and said, 'Murray, I never saw you again after the battle, for I was sent home. But thank you so much for saving my life. Upon my word, what a small world it really is!'

His eyes were well-ringed saucers as he said, 'Bless you, Doctor, you really need to thank old Captain here for that. My word, it is good to see you, and looking so well too. Whatever brings you to this quiet place, sir?'

As I fondled the old cab horse that had evidently saved my life, I explained that Holmes and I were looking for the toll bridge at Dolphin's Spine. Murray opened the door of his elderly vehicle and bade us to climb aboard. He grunted kindly to the horse, which needed no whip or harsh words to do his bidding.

Some ten minutes later the vehicle came to a halt as we saw the notice 'Toll One Half-Penny'. We decided to dispense with Murray and Captain and to continue on foot, having been assured by Murray that we could always find him near the station should we need to use his services. It was difficult enough to get him to accept the normal fare from us, let alone the sovereign which Holmes insisted on pressing upon him, insisting that in saving my life, Murray and Captain had possibly saved his own.

We looked around us with interest. On the side of the bridge at which we stood there was an inn, the Jolly Smugglers, surrounded by a few cottages and a general store. On the far side we could see the huge sandbank, which looked for all the world like the upper half of a dolphin, dotted with a number of shanties of the kind which in India we would have called bungalows. These abodes were surrounded with shingle gardens, if such they could be called, with rough fencing between these properties. There were, I estimated, about a dozen such buildings altogether, with some variation in size and state of repair. Some of the bungalows looked extremely run down. In the front of one of these stood a young man in a reefer jacket and wearing a yachting cap. He seemed to be observing us through a small glass or telescope, so at such a distance he could see a lot more of us than we could of him, for he stood a couple of hundred yards from us. Evidently having satisfied his curiosity he retreated into his dwelling.

Holmes decided that we should perhaps put up at the inn. We both had a few necessities of life with us and there seemed little sense in returning to Baker Street having found the place that we were seeking. We entered the main bar of the Jolly Smugglers and refreshed ourselves with tankards of local ale, and fortified our inner-men with bread and cheese. The landlord was not a jolly soul but we were not seeking entertainment, just accommodation. He had two rooms, indifferent but serviceable.

He handed us the keys and enquired, 'You gents wouldn't be here for the fishing, for you have no tackle and you are both pale of complexion. Forgive me for being nosey, but we are all a bit nosey round here, especially regarding strangers. You see, most of us are descended from the smugglers!'

Holmes quite surprised me with his reply. 'Quite so, landlord, and old habits die hard, even taking many generations to do so. I know the south coast well, and there are many old smugglers' inns where the atmosphere lingers on. Rest assured, sir, we are not excise men or indeed men with any kind of official authority. No, we are just gentlemen of leisure, seeking a young lady with whom we lost contact a while ago. I imagine you get to know, or at least hear about, most of the people who stay in this area. The lady we are seeking is possibly no longer staying here, but was of striking appearance, wearing rather distinctive clothes, leg of mutton sleeves, for example.'

I noticed a glint in the publican's eye and could tell that Holmes had struck some kind of a hit. The fellow paused, however, before he spoke, but when he did it was with a rather confidential air.

'It so happens that a very distinguished-looking young woman wearing such a style in clothing came in here about a month ago. I remember remarking to wife that her clothes, whilst of fine quality, were not of a style that one would expect to see worn by a woman of her age group. Why, my wife stopped wearing those leg of muttons years ago, and this, sir, is not exactly the centre of fashion! She came in to ask if she might have a pail of fresh water. Said that she and her husband had come to stay at *Mon Repos*, which is one of the bungalows just over the bridge, but that the water had not yet been reconnected. Naturally we let her have it and I remarked to my wife that her husband should have been the one to fetch the water.'

Holmes looked at him keenly. 'Did you see the husband?'

'Why, yes, he came in for a glass of ale the following day. I knew it was him because he thanked me for letting his wife have the water. Strange sort of chap he was, very slight. If it had not been for his rather luxuriant moustache, I would have said that he looked, well how shall I say, rather delicate? He wore a very large hat pulled down to his ears. Strange sort of chap, but a pleasant enough manner. He's been in several times since, and until a week or so ago his wife used to look in, usually for information or to borrow this or that.'

I asked a rather obvious question. 'Did they not come here together at any time?'

The publican scratched his head and then said, 'Why no, sir, come to think of it they never did. Never thought of that before. Tell you something else though, I did notice that their features had a certain similarity, but I put it down to them not being from round here. You know how people in certain districts do tend to look rather alike. It's the same round here, sir, with all those descended from the smugglers having certain similarity of features.'

We retreated to a table in a deserted corner of the bar where we sat and nursed our tankards. Holmes, already bristling with suppressed excitement as I might have expected in earlier days, spoke with interest concerning what he had heard.

'A couple, much of an age, with similarity of features, yet evidently husband and wife, have taken a bungalow in a secluded place. Of course they could be cousins, even brother and sister, posing as husband and wife for reasons of their own. She, although not yet middle-aged, wears clothes of a style more suited to dear Mrs Hudson. Both have been seen here a number of times, yet never together. Normally I would find none of this of particular or urgent interest, Watson, but coupled with the bloodstained dress of similar style and the likewise stained butcher's knife, and the toll ticket, I feel I am entitled to show some interest in the matter.'

I concurred, and reminded him of the young man who had viewed us from one of the bungalows through an optical glass. We decided to take a quiet stroll and make an early start with our investigations on the morrow. As we wandered the lane and smoked our pipes we, of course, discussed all that had occurred since my finding the luggage ticket upon the ground in Regent's Park. Holmes was positively enigmatic as he spoke.

'It is, Watson, just as if destiny, fate or whatever you wish to call it, had decided to pose this puzzling series of events to lure me back to my destiny, aye, and perhaps save my sanity in the doing. The chance meeting with the man whose horse saved your own life was also rather dramatic. Upon my word, Watson, I am beginning to feel as if we are both pawns in some all-powerful One's game!'

# CHAPTER 3

# The Residents of *Mon Repos*

It was at about eleven of the clock on the following morning that we stood before the gate of *Mon Repos* prior to our very first direct approach to contact with that residence's occupants. The young gentleman we had seen before only from a distance stood upon his own side of the gate. At least, I assumed that it was the same man, and he had doubtless seen us coming toward the building from quite a distance, for he could from his window see the bridge and even the inn, and we knew that he was inclined to use field glasses.

He was smartly dressed in a neat grey suit and I was struck by how very slim he appeared to be, even for a man in his late twenties or early thirties as I took him for. He had a luxuriant auburn moustache, matching the tone of his hair, or that of it which could be seen from beneath the soft hat which was pulled well down. With large bright eyes he surveyed us from beneath the brim of his hat, addressing us, speaking softly but firmly.

'Gentlemen, can I assist you in some way?' The question was a natural one to ask of two strangers who stood before one's garden gate. (I use the word 'garden' loosely, because the *Mon Repos* surround could scarcely be thus described, being mainly sand and shingle with the few plants that had prospered being of a marine nature.) Holmes took the initiative.

'Sir, my name is Horatio Reynolds and this is my colleague, Dr Mortimer Snipe. We are students of the flora and fauna of the seashore and we are seeking a bungalow in this area where we might be able to set up a small research headquarters. Perhaps you could tell me if there is anything of the kind that could be available in this vicinity?'

He replied, 'Well, it so happens that my wife and I are thinking of shortly vacating this bungalow. We rented it from a Mr Scrooby, an agent with premises in Trenchard Street. Pray come inside that I can give you some idea of its facilities. My name, by the way, is Dale Reiner. I am American but of Teutonic origin as my name will suggest to you.'

I took the chance to leap in where Holmes evidently did not wish to, and asked, 'Mr Reiner, is your wife at home at the present time?'

'Why no, Dr Snipe, did you particularly wish to meet her?'

Holmes jumped in at this point with, I thought, great presence of mind, saying, 'My colleague has found, as have I myself, from past experience that the lady of the house as a rule has the last word in the matter of vacating the premises.'

Reiner seemed to accept these words with good grace

and was affable enough to offer to show us over the bungalow. It proved to be typical of its kind, a rather basic timber
building, disguised with a shingle-dashed exterior and being
formed mainly of one large room with one or two extremely
small ones to each of its side. At the rear there was a
kitchen and the principal windows were to each side of the
front door which led directly into the main room as the
building boasted no entrance hall. One could tell from the
sparse cane furnishings that the premises were intended
and being in fact used as temporary accommodation. There
were no ornaments, few books and little that seemed connected with entertainment or any sort of a life of comfort.

Our host seemed to sense my impression, saying, 'Oh
yes, Doctor, it is indeed spartan but it serves our purpose.
In fact we have already stayed longer than we had intended.'

In one corner of the room there was a hat stand, bearing
a wide-brimmed gentleman's panama and a lady's sun hat
with an even broader brim and a decorative band. In an
adjacent umbrella stand there were several canes including
an ebony one and a malacca, plus a lady's sunshade covered
in purple silk. There were, too, several racquets for tennis
and lacrosse. In the far corner there stood a pile of trunks,
each bearing the initials 'I.A.'. Reiner noticed Holmes's
gimlet glance at these and answered his unspoken question.

'I imagine you find those initials upon the trunks rather
surprising given my own being "D.R."? Well, my wife and I
are not long wed and her maiden name was Iris Anderson.
We have been meaning to get the initials altered for ages as
they produce embarrassment when we stay at an hotel!'

He opened the side doors in turn to show us the anterooms. There was a bedroom with a single bed and a dressing table but no wardrobe, rather a fair number of women's dresses hanging upon a stand. Another door was opened to reveal some items of garden furniture whilst the third had a couch and a man's suit hanging from a hook on the door back. The last room proved to be almost entirely filled with musical items, a small upright piano and a table piled with musical scores.

'I am a composer, Mr Reynolds, and I work in this room. I believe this place would suit your purpose from the little you have told me. The main room could become a laboratory and the others for living accommodation. There are outbuildings for storage. My wife could give you more information regarding the running of the place, hiring domestics and so on. She will return tomorrow, so why do you not call again at about midday?'

We promised to do so and he shook hands with us both in a candid manner. He had small, slim fingers, yet a firm handshake.

As we walked back across the shaky bridge, Holmes remarked, 'An extremely polite and artistic young man, as one might expect of a composer. I noticed that he had few possessions; most items that were there appeared to be hers, save for a spare suit of clothes and a cane or two. Why even the trunks were hers. Did you particularly notice anything else, Watson?'

'Yes, he kept his hat on, pulled well down, even inside the bungalow.'

'What significance did you place upon that?'

'He could have lost his hair through accident or illness

and be awaiting its regrowth. Otherwise he could belong to some strict religious sect requiring the head to be covered at all times?'

'I like your second reason best, for what hair could be seen beneath the hat brim seemed to be healthy. But I am not entirely happy with either deduction, Watson.'

'I imagine you accepted his reason for the initials "I.A." being painted upon the trunks?'

'Oh yes, Watson, but how about the domestic arrangements? She has a bedroom but he has only a couch and a few hangers. His music room, he explains on account of his being a composer. Yet I saw no sign of writing materials or manuscript paper, save that already written or printed upon, the works of classic originators. Had he told me that he was a singer I would have been happier with what I saw.'

'But how can any of this affect our main purpose of investigation, the possible murder of a woman at *Mon Repos* in the recent past?'

Holmes smiled enigmatically before he spoke. 'There may be a connection, Watson, there well may be a connection. I would remind you that we have not yet set eyes upon Mrs Reiner, née Iris Anderson. Mr Reiner may well give some excuse for her non-appearance on the morrow. Indeed I will be a trifle surprised if we do meet her.'

'But, Holmes, surely he would not have suggested that we visit again tomorrow, expressly to meet her, if it were not possible to arrange?'

He nodded. 'We shall see, Watson, he may have been playing for time. Tomorrow, who knows, perhaps we will find an empty bungalow?'

As it happens this was not to be so, but then I must not jump the gun, as we used to say in the army, and will come to that circumstance in its due turn.

Meanwhile Holmes continued, 'I think that a visit to Mr Scrooby, the owner of the bungalow, might prove profitable. I believe Reiner mentioned that his office was in Trenchard Street?'

It was not difficult to find that thoroughfare in a place so small and Scrooby & Co. was patently the place of business of an agent dealing in properties and residences, his own and those of others. Mr Scrooby had one of those names to suit his visage, as Dickens might have put it. He was tall, thin and sparse of locks, with those that remained to him being carefully pomaded and arranged over his high brow.

'Mr Reynolds, Dr Snipe, my secretary informs me that you are seeking premises in the area? Well, you have come to the right place, the best place, in fact the *only* place in the area dealing in desirable property. What sort of accommodation did you have in mind?'

He rubbed his hands together in a gesture reminiscent of Uriah Heep. Holmes continued the deception of the characters and occupations that he had invented for us. 'We are scientists, sir, studying the flora and fauna of the southern British coast. We mean to establish a small research headquarters and have seen a property, which I understand belongs to your good self, a bungalow called . . . what was it called, my dear Snipe?'

'Why, er, I believe it is titled *Mon Repos*!'

I played my part in a manner which I hoped was worthy of Sir Henry Irving, given the inspiration of Holmes's masterly characterisation of a vague academic. Holmes carried the scene to its purpose.

'Quite so, *Mon Repos*! A splendid site for our work. You know, Mr Scrooby, there is a marine weed only to be found on this part of the coast, and I have noticed how very quiet the spot is which would suit us perfectly. I imagine it is perhaps beyond our slender purse strings, however?'

To see and hear Sherlock Holmes playing Scrooby like a wily fish was a lesson to me and a reassurance concerning the recovery of his mental powers. At once the agent was ready to give Holmes the information he required without suspecting the real requirement purpose.

'Oh Mr Reynolds, I feel sure we can come to an arrangement. You see the property is at present let only at popular times of the year to those who seek the sun and sea bathing. But a permanent occupant could find me very cooperative indeed. The present occupants have been there only a few weeks. A quiet couple, a Mr and Mrs Reiner from the United States. I have met only the husband but my staff have called there for the rent and dealt with Mrs Reiner and reported that she is as seemingly respectable as he. Before the Reiners it was unoccupied for a time, and a somewhat unsuitable tenant stayed there for a while. A single gentleman, but we had to ask him to leave because a woman, evidently other than his wife or a relative, stayed there with him occasionally. But although she evidently left after a few days I had to ask him for the keys. One cannot be too careful. Why, we let a bungalow to an actress once, or rather she described herself as such, but between ourselves I discovered that she was,' he lowered his voice, '. . . a music-hall artiste!'

We both clicked our tongues in suitable concern, then Holmes looked carefully at an offer written upon a scrap of paper and we promised to consider this. Scrooby bowed us out and we waited until we were well out of earshot before we discussed what we had learned.

I said, 'So Scrooby has actually had contact with Mrs Reiner, Holmes, even if only through his underlings. At least we know that she exists!'

But he corrected me. 'Existed, Watson, existed! We are concerned, are we not, with her present existence?'

This I had to concede. After all, the tragedy concerning the bloodstained dress and the butcher's knife could have been of an extremely recent nature. As we returned to the inn we passed the bridge and gazed across to see the distant figure of Mr Dale Reiner with his field glasses trained upon us, or to be more accurate trained upon the general area within which we strolled. In my almost permanent role as devil's advocate I remarked that he might be an ornithologist.

Holmes chuckled. 'You could be right, Watson, the gentleman has told us that he is a composer. Yet there is no known law that forbids a musical scholar from studying bird life!'

My life has been full of surprises, as any reader of my past chronicles of my adventures with Sherlock Holmes will appreciate. But the midday hour of the day which followed provided me with one of the greatest of these. I had said little to Holmes about it, but in my mind and in fact deep down in my heart lay a deep suspicion that Mrs

Reiner no longer existed. I had in fact suffered a nightmare in which Holmes and I sat bound and gagged whilst Dale Reiner murdered her with a butcher's knife in front of our helpless eyes. Of course there had been nothing in Reiner's manner or appearance to suggest that he was other than an extremely respectable and artistic young American, but the mind does indeed play tricks during slumber. Yet when we were met at the gate by a slender woman in a black dress and veil, as if she were in mourning, I was very surprised, especially as there was something about her to suggest the Black Widow of my encounter in Regent's Park.

'Mr Reynolds, Dr Snipe, good morning. My name is Iris Reiner. I was away from home attending my late and favourite aunt's funeral when you called yesterday. This sad event will explain my veil, but she was a dear soul and I have been saddened more than I can say.'

We shook hands with the lady, reassuring her concerning the veil and gladly accepting her invitation to enter and partake of coffee. As she poured it, thick and black, she showed that she had a sense of humour, despite her obvious American origin. 'I hope coffee is to your liking. We don't care for tea. Mind, having tasted what passes for coffee in this little old country, I can well understand how you prefer tea!'

I noticed that her voice was very husky, and she explained this by saying that she had contracted laryngitis through the harsh climate of the seashore.

I gave her my professional advice. 'You should gargle with port wine, Mrs Reiner. Opera singers swear by it:

Jenny Lind would go nowhere without a bottle of the Portuguese grape!'

She was grateful for the advice. 'I did not realize that you were a doctor of medicine, sir. I move in a world where doctorates can represent the unexpected.'

Of course I had slipped up in falling into what might have been a trap, although I did not suspect that it was. But Holmes glared at me and I left the talking to him for the most part thereafter. He made polite enquiries concerning the local postal service, domestic arrangements, and enquired about much that I was aware that he already knew. But this gave me a chance to observe the lady carefully, despite her veil, and a rather wild theory began to form in my mind to the extent that I was anxious to inform Holmes of my wild thoughts.

We made our farewells with the lady, as she thanked me again for the vocal advice and then we made our way back across the bridge toward the inn.

As we walked I began to speak my mind. 'Holmes, I wonder if the same wild thought has occurred to you as it has to me. Could it be that although we have seemed to meet both Reiners, we have in fact met but one of them?'

'Something of the kind had occurred to me, Watson. I am suspicious that only one Reiner seems to be there when we call. I have felt the possibility of an impersonation and I would be glad to hear of any thoughts that you have upon the possibility.'

'Well, I felt that her excuse for the wearing of the heavy veil was a thin one. The mourning clothes I could understand, but why would she wear the veil in the confines of her own home. Moreover, in her widow's weeds she looked exactly like the mysterious woman that I saw in Regent's Park, the one who started this whole episode! There was also, I noticed, even in spite of the veil, a certain similarity of features between the two of them. All of this leads me to believe, strange and bizarre as it may seem, that Reiner impersonated for our benefit his non-existent wife, existent no more on account of his having murdered her.'

We had reached the entrance to the inn so we dropped our voices and did not continue to discuss the matter until we were safely ensconced in an alcove of the private bar, away from the possibility of being overhead. Then, over the top of a pewter tankard, it was Sherlock Holmes who spoke first.

'An interesting slant upon a theory which in essence I have myself in mind. You imagine, then, that Reiner took on the role of female impersonator when interviewing us, complete with dress and veil? I too had noticed, despite the intervening muslin, a certain likeness of features more to be expected in a brother and sister rather than in husband and wife. However, I take a different interpretation of this to your own. I believe, Watson, that whilst indeed only one Reiner is involved, that Reiner is female. The Black Widow is an impersonation of course, but needing far less disguise than her other role as Dale Reiner!'

His words surprised me to say the very least. Of course I had seen music-hall artistes who were male impersonators, for example a Miss Ella Shields. But to carry such an impersonation into a world outside of the theatre seemed far fetched.

I protested, but was merely clutching at straws. 'How about that luxuriant moustache?'

'False. I even remember detecting a whiff of spirit gum. I thought little of it at the time but now, of course, it falls into place.'

'How about the hair?'

'My dear fellow, do you not remember that Mr Reiner wore a soft hat, pulled well down even inside the bunga-low? We remarked upon it after that first visit.'

I was forced to agree to his theory, or rather at least in its possibility. But of course it did put a rather different com-plexion on things.

'Does this mean, Holmes, that we are now on the trail of a murderess rather than a murderer?'

He looked unusually thoughtful by even his own stand-ards as he replied, 'However unlikely the thought might seem, Watson, I do not discount it, no, I do not discount it!'

Of course, reasons for his version of events that being true ones did occur to me. For example, if the person involved was in fact a woman why had she taken so much trouble to establish both male and female versions of her persona locally, and why had she sported her male character disguise whilst watching us with field glasses soon after our arrival.

I voiced these questions and Holmes simply replied, 'I don't know, Watson, as yet I do not know. But I do know that she was expecting us.'

At this point we took luncheon which the landlord provided: cold cuts of mutton with mashed potatoes and beetroot followed by a good suet pudding with treacle.

Afterwards Holmes sensed that I was a little drowsy. He put the thought into words.

'My dear Watson, I need to give this whole problem my undivided attention. It may even be a three- or four-pipe problem, so I suggest that you go to your room and take a nap, an hour or so. I will need at least that long and will see you back in this bar at about five of the clock.'

# CHAPTER 4

# The Great Impersonation

Promptly at five, having rested rather than slept, I joined Holmes in the bar, where I found him seated with pad and pencil, seeming to be trying to make an anagram of the letters of the name Dale Reiner. He had written some extremely unlikely examples upon the pad, including Reed Linder, Earl Denier and Reni Dealer. There were many other examples which made no sense.

He brightened as he greeted me, saying, 'Come, Watson, sit a moment and prepare yourself for yet another expedition to *Mon Repos*. I believe I know the true identity of Mrs Reiner, as we have known her, and I think you are in for a considerable surprise should my belief regarding her identity prove to be correct.'

I did not at that moment in time press Holmes for more information, knowing how he loved to lay his cards gently, slowly and in their turn upon the table. No good could ever come of placing pressure upon Sherlock Holmes, who would always follow his own paths and in his own good time. However, as we set out for yet another visit to *Mon Repos* I could not help but wish that he would tell me what to expect, or rather *who* to expect.

As we stood before the gate to the path up to the doorway of that rather dilapidated residence I fancied I caught the flutter of a curtain at the window, and so assumed that whoever was within knew well that we were present. Holmes stood there, his tall frame erect, his head thrown back like some gigantic heron, the likeness emphasized by his great beak of a nose. I had never seen him appear to be more alert or more healthful, at least for a man of his intemperate habits. Whilst I felt some anxiety as to what might happen next, I felt secure in the justification of my action that had led to our present position. Where I had feared for my friend's life I no longer did so, save through some more dangerous turn of events, for I had not with me my service revolver.

Holmes took a deep breath and then he spoke loudly and clearly rather than shouted. 'Miss Adler, you may come out now, and show yourself without need of your veil!'

There was a silence lasting about ten seconds before the front door of *Mon Repos* opened to reveal, framed like an exquisite full-length painting, the classic form and features of none other than *the* woman, Irene Adler! I had not set eyes upon her since a time when she had almost caused, but for the intervention of Sherlock Holmes, a scandal in bohemia. Of course I knew that Holmes had encountered her since then, during that period of his disappearance and widely believed death connected with the Reichenbach Falls. I knew little of the details save that she had been of great assistance to him in evading the henchmen of the infamous and far from lamented Professor Moriarty. She was as beautiful as I remembered her, and spoke in her pleasing American tones, unhampered by the laryingitis for which I had prescribed a port gargle.

'My dear Sherlock, how nice it is to see you again, and to perceive that you have recovered your health. I could not of course remark upon this during your visits to me in my roles as husband and wife. Dr Watson, it is good to see you too. Pray will you both be so kind as to enter?'

I followed Holmes into the bungalow in a sort of haze. I could not believe that the widow had been the adorable Irene, or more to the point, that she could have been involved in the wrongdoing that we were investigating. She sat us at a low table, afternoon tea already arranged, as if we had been expected.

Holmes was the first of the two of us to speak. 'My dear Miss Adler, does it surprise you that I penetrated the two personas that you have recently adopted?'

'My dear Sherlock, the answer is both yes and no. I had expected you to see through all of my ruses sooner or later, but not quite this soon. I played the game, I did not cheat, I left you some clues of the kind which I knew only an intellect such as yours could have picked up on. Tell me, was it the anagram of my name that finally gave me away?'

Of course! Even I could see that Dale Reiner was an anagram of Irene Adler, even without the use of pencil and pad, but only now that the fact had been suggested to me. Evidently Holmes had fallen in to this earlier in the day. But what were the other clues that she had mentioned leaving? I made so bold as to enquire concerning these. Her reply was a masterpiece of concise explanation.

'Well, the presentation of male and female characters, evidently husband and wife yet never seen together either by yourselves or anyone else in this district must have made for suspicion. The hat which hid my hair, or most of it, and the moustache which was agony to wear must surely have seemed strange. The heavily veiled woman, presenting an appearance bizarre unless made at a funeral or very soon after? Come, Doctor, I knew that all these things would be well noted. Oh and of course, Doctor, you had seen the Black Widow before, when she dropped the left luggage receipt in the park. I had known when I dropped it that you would be unable to resist claiming my hat box and presenting your ailing friend with a possibly life-saving problem. Some supernumeries in my little drama played thug and cab driver.'

Sherlock Holmes had listened to her narration like a man in a dream, yet one that was engrossing and without the terror of a nightmare.

After taking a sip of her imported American tea and asking her permission to do so, he lit an Egyptian cigarette and said, 'I may have been clear concerning your identity for a matter of hours and your actions for a matter of days, but I might as well own that your motives elude me utterly and completely. After all, you have gone to a great deal of trouble not to mention expense in leading me such a chase. You have hired a bungalow, travelled extensively and planted clues that must have taxed your wits and ingenuity. The hat box, I imagine, was your own, but you hired cabs, actors to play parts, and obtained artefacts including a toll ticket, a bloodstained woman's dress and a knife that had probably been used to kill its wearer.'

Irene started slightly before she replied. 'My dear Sherlock, your first question answers itself by your very presence here, so well and alert. I had heard of your illness and the nature of it and that nothing seemed to help you, my poor friend. I decided that only a really intriguing enigma of the kind that only you could be likely to solve might effect the cure. It had to be planted, in such a way that it would intrigue first your fine friend, Dr Watson, and in turn yourself. I colluded with your splendid brother, Mycroft, who helped me with some of the details and with the financial aspect. But now I come to an angle of your questions which troubles me. To quote you, I believe you said that the owner of the bloodstained woman's dress was probably killed with the butcher's knife?'

Holmes blew blue smoke from his cigarette. 'First, may I express my gratitude for your concern for my well-being. Though at first tempted to be petty and ask, "Who asked for your interference?" But yes, that would be petty indeed and I do appreciate your friendly concern. However, now to a more serious matter. Where did you obtain the knife and the bloodstained garment?'

'When I hired this bungalow from Scrooby, the knife was in a drawer with other kitchen implements ancient and modern. As for the dress, I found it screwed up and stuffed under a cushion in this bungalow. I assumed that some previous occupant had spilled some blood down her dress whilst preparing a meal. I thought that providentially it went rather well with the butcher's knife to form clues in my false trail. I did not associate the items with each other, nor even assume that they had figured in any sort of crime!'

Holmes looked more than a little thoughtful for a minute or so, before he spoke again. When he did there was a sort of suppressed excitement of the games-afoot variety in his voice.

'So, my dear Miss Adler, in inventing and manufacturing clues for a spurious crime you have unearthed some articles connected with a real one. I do congratulate you, for you have done better than you expected to or even intended.'

Miss Adler and I exchanged a glance. We both obviously had the same kind of thought, the question in our minds being would Holmes now call it a day and leave any real crime to the police, or would he continue to follow up on what now had become quite a bizarre affair.

Soon Sherlock answered our unasked question. 'Miss Adler, Watson, perhaps it was fate that brought us all together in this affair which to you, dear lady, has taken an unexpected turn. Therefore, I feel bound to continue with my investigations into something which you had contrived without realizing its full implications. Watson, would you be so kind as to return to the inn and fetch from my room a small leather Gladstone bag which you will easily find. It contains not only the suspect knife and blood-stained dress, but a number of those tools of my trade which are, as with your stethoscope, usually to be found wherever I may be, especially if I am likely to be away from home for more than a few hours. At least . . .' (he hesitated) 'at least this was always so before my retirement, and fortunately for this present expedition I have taken again to old habits.'

Returning to the inn I quickly found the Gladstone bag but did not immediately set off back to the bungalow. Instead I smoked a pipe of tobacco and partook of a tankard of ale in the bar. The reader will, I feel sure, hardly need to be told that it was not sloth which prompted this behaviour; rather did I feel that Holmes might want the opportunity to converse with his old friendly adversary, Irene Adler. When I did set out to return, however, I still took the walk slowly in order to enjoy the fresh sea air and think about the strange events that had led us to meet with her again. Miss Adler and Mycroft had taken such a lot of trouble to plant this irresistible crime and she had appeared truly amazed to learn that Holmes considered a real crime to be involved. Yet, ah yet, with minds as canny as hers and Mycroft's, how could I be sure that we were not still following a false trail. But, I thought, surely Holmes would soon learn of it if this were so.

'My dear fellow, you have indeed taken your time. No matter, Miss Adler and I have taken the opportunity to have a long and earnest conversation regarding the events of the years since last we met. Time is kind to some of us, Watson, is it not?'

I felt it was the gentlemanly thing for me to say, 'In Miss Adler's case it is certainly true, for she looks not a day older than when last we were involved, whilst I fear that I have aged a great deal since that time.'

Her reply was kindly in the extreme. 'Doctor, you simply look a little more distinguished.'

Holmes spoiled it all by insisting upon informing us both that distinguished was from the French, and in that language meant old!

'Come, Watson, we have dallied long enough with pleasantries and must get to work. Hand me the bag, there's a good fellow.'

I did as I was bade and he opened the well-worn case almost with a flourish. He spread first the gruesome dress upon a chairback and then took forth the bloodstained knife which he placed upon the table. He followed this by fetching from the bag an extremely large and powerful lens and a series of tweezers. On display these gruesome objects looked like part of the Black Museum at Scotland Yard!

But I expressed rather more practical thoughts. 'Approximately how long ago do you imagine this tragedy to have occurred?'

He shrugged. 'It is difficult to say with any exactitude. The blood is well dried into the cloth, but the material is still stiff with it. Observations past have shown me that such stiffness would have been mellowed by time. Perhaps a year, or a little more, and the blood on the knife which matches it shows signs of being more recent than the animal blood which is also present.'

He spread the dress, holding it up to the light. 'Have you any observations upon the garment, Watson, for until now we have given it but passing attention?'

I took his lens and examined the gown with renewed interest. 'Well, I can only add the thought that we might be looking at signs of a tragedy other than murder: that of suicide. Could the poor woman not have taken her own life by thrusting the knife point into her throat, or just below it? Perhaps she was attempting to push it through the opening below the front of the collar, missing by an inch or so and producing the bloodsoaked tear.'

Holmes as ever damned me with faint praise. 'A splendid thought, Watson, concerning the attention to make use of that opening at the top of the dress. Whoever wielded the knife probably did so with shaking hand and missed the target. But as for your suicide theory, I am amazed that it should spring from the lips of a medical man. There are many easier places to damage onself if intent upon ending one's life than the site chosen. The heart perhaps? But with a woman involved the most usual thing to find would be severed arteries, at the wrist or ankle. Nonetheless, I think you are right when you hint that we may not be looking at signs of murder.'

I could not follow his train of thought. 'If not suicide or murder, then surely only self-defence can be the motive?'

But Sherlock Holmes would not be drawn further upon the subject at that particular point in time.

'We need more to go on than just the bloodstained clothing and the butcher's knife. This place in which we presently stand may well be the scene of tragedy, whatever form it might have taken. Let us look then for further evidence. I would like, Miss Adler, to see the drawer from which you took the knife.'

She took us to the kitchen and indicated the drawer which he opened and examined. There appeared to be little in the drawer to strike interest or connection. It was empty save for a ball of twine and a few pins. Holmes closed it and proceeded to open other drawers in the room to observe their contents. The bungalow was equipped with only the most basic items, and not intended to do more than satisfy a simple way of living. There were a few knives and forks of the table variety and a simple Welsh dresser with plates and cups. Holmes seemed to find little to interest him in the kitchen save the scrubbed table top. He pointed to it dramatically.

'Beds aside, this table is about the only surface in the bungalow large enough and suitable to lay a body upon. Its top has been scrubbed very thoroughly, to an extent of cleanliness not found elsewhere in the building. Notice also that the sides have been scrubbed, which is unusual even where the housekeeper is more than fastidious.'

I followed his pointing finger with my eyes and observed that indeed the four-inch planks which spanned the legs just below the table top had indeed been scoured but could not quite follow the significance of this. Holmes enlarged upon his theme by turning the table up onto one of its short ends.

'Whoever scrubbed the table and its sides failed to think of cleaning the underside. Observe bloodstains on the under-edges of the side planks. The dry wood has even attracted this blood up and under.'

He took his lens to these stains and then his penknife to scrape some of them, dropping these minute shavings into small envelopes from his Gladstone.

There was satisfaction rather than triumph in his voice as he said, 'I'll wager we shall find this blood to match that upon the stained garments. I am convinced that the unfortunate woman, the victim of this tragedy, was laid upon this table whilst another person, stronger than she, used the knife upon her.'

I replied to this rather warmly. 'So you have changed your mind regarding it being a case of murder?'

His reply puzzled me. 'Certainly not. The woman could have been treated by a person hardly qualified to do so, under conditions of secrecy. Something obviously went terribly wrong and perhaps the patient, if she can be so called, possibly died. Of course we cannot be sure at this stage.'

'You mean . . .' I cast a quick glance at Miss Adler before I continued to speak, but she smiled reassuringly at me and said, 'Dr Watson, you were about to use the word abortion, were you not? Pray do not be coy on my account, for this appears to be a serious matter.'

I nodded. 'The thought had occurred to me.'

But Holmes did not seem to be of quite the same mind. 'Not necessarily an abortion, but any operation is illegal if performed by one unqualified.'

I said, 'He took a lot of trouble over scrubbing the table, yet Miss Adler found the bloodstained dress under a cushion and the knife in a drawer. Would these items not have been disposed of?'

'Quite so and doubtless their careful disposal was intended, but he might well have been disturbed and forced to leave very suddenly.'

The whole gruesome picture of he who had performed some illegal operation having disposed of the body, scrubbed the table upon which he had operated, having only time to hide rather than dispose of the knife and clothing. Perhaps the police were at his very door. Holmes did not dwell upon that which we had discussed but rather busied himself in searching every nook and cranny of the bungalow. He found little to interest himself save a single leather glove which had a portion of one of its fingers trimmed away with some sharp instrument at its very tip. He added this to his library of clues.

Sherlock Holmes decided at this point to pause and charge his pipe, saying to Irene, 'My dear Miss Adler, I do not normally smoke strong tobacco when there is a lady present. However, my grey matter does not operate to its maximum extent without it and I have reached a point where I need to be left to my own devices and to my Lady Nicotine. Might I suggest that Watson accompanies you upon a pleasant stroll for the next two hours as I will be poor company whilst meditating to consider all that we have learned?'

Miss Adler took a firm hold upon my arm as she said, 'My dear Sherlock, despite my vocation strong tobacco fumes do not worry me, indeed I am known to smoke the odd cheroot myself! However, I appreciate that you wish to be left in peace for a couple of hours. Come, Doctor, please take me for the stroll that your friend suggests.'

We strolled the length of the Dolphin's Spine in both directions, and then crossed the bridge back to the village. We did not make for the inn because Miss Adler would have felt uncomfortable in the bar parlour and could hardly be seen to accompany me to my room. Instead we made for the only café in the vicinity, which was quite a fifteen-minute walk. As we made for this eating place, Miss Adler entertained me with her bright chatter.

'I have been into the inn of course, Doctor, but only in my character as Dale Reiner. My ability to carry off male impersonations has stood me in good stead through the years, both privately and professionally. I have even had offers to play Prince Charming at the Lyceum pantomime.' (She gave me an example of her attractive and merry laugh.) 'I turned it down, but if I were to be offered Aladdin, I might be tempted!'

We sat at a secluded table in the corner of the far from fashionable café and I ordered some tea and pastries, the hour being about midway between luncheon and dinner. An elderly waitress in a uniform which scarcely flattered her, giving the impression of mutton dressed as lamb, brought us our tea and cakes with rather poor grace.

I remarked to Miss Adler concerning the waitress's lack of catering expertise, but as ever she was kindly in her reply.

'My dear Doctor, she is a lady of indeterminate age and probably has no husband to support her, certainly she wears no wedding band upon her fingers, so we must allow her a certain measure of grumpiness.'

I noticed thereafter that she was very gentle in her tones and actions when dealing with the lady and quite won her over by the time we made to depart. However, before then we discussed everything that we knew of the *Mon Repos* affair filling each other in upon missing details.

'Miss Adler, oh dash it, might I call you Irene? I am amazed at the complexity of the plot that you hatched with Mycroft.'

'Of course you may, John, and yes, I suppose we did go to a great deal of trouble, but then our dear friend's recovery was worth any amount of effort. So you were completely taken in with my impersonation of the Black Widow?'

'Yes, and also with the bogus cab and footpad. You must have known that once at Victoria it would take that little extra push to go through with my deception?'

'Of course. Everything worked according to plan save in the selection of those items from the bungalow. I had no idea that I was presenting Sherlock with clues to a real crime. Do you think he is as yet up to solving it?'

'He is up to it I believe, but I wonder if it really is a crime. Perhaps it is all the result of some emergency treatment to an injured woman.'

Irene fixed me with her limpid gaze. 'He will know, my dear John, by the time we return.'

Almost exactly two hours later Irene and I returned to *Mon Repos*, having achieved very little save the Christian name terms which we now enjoyed. Holmes appeared to be exactly where we had left him and surrounded by the tools of his trade and of his addictions. But that he had not moved since we had left him I doubted, and would have done even without the bootmarks in the circle of tobacco ash. He looked up at us from the cushion upon the floor on which he was seated.

He was more communicative than when we had left him. 'My dear Miss Adler, Watson, pray be seated for I have to tell you of progress made.'

'So, you have advanced with your investigative thoughts, Holmes? I am delighted to hear it.'

Irene and I took cushions from the chairs and seated ourselves beside him on the floor, as near to him as the surrounding collection of objects would allow. He glanced at us in turn, something near to triumph in his expression.

'After long thought and deliberation I believe that no murder was involved here, but a crime took place in that the authorities were not informed of events, some of which were certainly illegal. I had assumed something of the sort, as indeed I imagine you must have, after we discovered that the kitchen table had clearly been used for some kind of operation. For a time I played with the idea that it might have concerned firearms. If the woman had been shot, even accidentally, medical attention of an unofficial nature might have been involved if the firearm responsible was held without licence or permit. For example, Watson, as an ex-army officer you carry permission to own a service revolver and if one of the three of us were to be injured accidentally by it there would be no point in concealing the fact by not seeking proper medical attention. But if you held that revolver illegally, there might be incentive to hide the facts. Imagine if you were not a doctor and attempted to minister medical assistance yourself.'

Having more or less made a good case for a firearm being involved, Holmes had in the same breath said that he did not believe this to be so.

I was puzzled, therefore, by his train of thought and said as much. 'First you tell us that it was probably not an accident with a firearm, then you tell us how easily it could have been. Really, Holmes, I do not follow!'

He smiled and nodded. 'Quite so, I will make myself clear. My parables concerning firearms were just suggesting a train of thought. What other reason could there be for

urgent medical treatment to be given to a woman by someone in this bungalow. Let us suppose that the woman was
with child but unmarried, and fearful of her condition
being made public.'

'But, Holmes, we did suggest abortion, yet you dis-
counted it.'

'Exactly, I did and I do. You see among the bizarre
objects that I discovered in one of the drawers was a leather
glove with a portion of one of the fingertips neatly removed.
How would you account for this?'

'It could have been used by someone who needed to
extend the tip of a finger . . . like the mittens worn by
people who need to count banknotes under freezing conditions.'

Holmes gave me a pitying look, and Irene also appeared
unconvinced by my words. 'My dear John, it doesn't seem
very likely.'

Holmes chuckled. 'It seemed to me to be some sort of
makeshift method of feeding a baby, filtering milk into its
mouth through the glove in the absence of a proper feeding
bottle. The fact that no such utensil was available shows
that the birth was unexpected, at least by all save the
woman concerned. It was all a desperate emergency and I
imagine it ended in tragedy, with the death first of the
woman and later of the child.'

I could see a certain logicality in his story, but I felt that
I could shoot it full of holes. The most obvious of these
being concerned with the knife wound at the throat of the
victim.

'Holmes, I have delivered a great many children but have

never stabbed the mother-to-be in the throat with a butcher's knife!'

He looked pityingly at me as he explained, as if speaking to an idiot, 'No, Watson, of course not, but it may be that you have never found it necessary to perform a tracheotomy to counteract a breathing crisis on the mother-to-be's part?'

'Why no, although I have performed that operation often enough, but not, I grant, you through a birth complication.'

'Exactly. The frantic man attempted such a practice in order to prevent the patient expiring through a blockage of the larynx or pharynx. He had no surgical implements and used the point of the butcher's knife in sheer desperation, possibly killing the already choking woman in the process. He managed to deliver the child, however, or he would not have needed to make that feeding device. I would like your further comments.'

'Well, Holmes, I can see possibility in your theory.' He started at my use of the word! 'I can only say that despite his use of makeshift means you must be looking for a man with some medical knowledge. Few laymen would have thought to try and perform a tracheotomy, even if the result was so tragic, and the glove device for feeding a child also suggests experience as well as ingenuity. However, I suggest that you cannot be sure that the mother and child perished.'

Holmes rose to his feet and walked toward the back door of the bungalow, beckoning to us to follow him. As we emerged into what could only loosely be referred to as a back garden (for it was of shingle and sand rather than grass and soil) he pointed dramatically, first to a short row of marine shrubs and then at a small clump of similar weed on the opposite side of the yard. There were other such rows and clumps of seashore growth and I could not quite see why he was indicating these particular plants.

But he explained. 'You will notice the clumps of weed I have pointed out to you have not flourished, or do not at this moment, to the extent that the others do, despite exactly similar conditions. I am not a gardener but I have studied botany, at least passingly, and I know that a plant does not prosper if dug up at the wrong time of year, even if immediately replanted as were these.'

I did not at once take his point, but Irene did. 'Sherlock, you mean that the bodies were buried at these sites, and the weeds replanted over them?'

'My dear Miss Adler, that is exactly what I mean!'

I looked long and hard at the two places where the weed had not prospered and I confess I shuddered at the thought of what must lay below, assuming Holmes's deductions were correct, and I had a growing feeling that they were.

'What must we do, Holmes, dig? I believe I noticed a spade around one side of the bungalow.'

'I think not, Watson. The time has sadly arrived where I have no alternative but to notify the authorities concerning our discoveries. I rather think that the pair of you, Miss Adler and yourself, have rather a lot of explaining to do!'

I started and replied, warmly, 'Oh, so you do not consider that you have yourself anything to answer for to the police?'

'Not at all, I am just a poor invalid, led astray by my

devious friends. Miss Adler will probably be deported, you, Watson, may end up in Dartmoor breaking stones, whilst Mycroft will almost certainly lose the trust of the King and his ministers!'

I was about to lose my temper with Sherlock Holmes for perhaps the first time ever, about to remark upon his ingratitude toward good friends whose only mistake had been to rescue him from a serious mental illness. Fortunately I caught the wicked gleam in his eyes and saw the corners of his mouth twitch with anticipated laughter in the nick of time. So instead I simply grunted before the three of us exploded into laughter that was immoderate to say the least.

It was eventually Irene who pulled us out of our merriment. 'Gentlemen, please! Whilst I realize that there is ironic humour in the situation, I would remind you that a woman and her child, according to Sherlock, lay buried in the garden of this bungalow. The woman may have been innocent of any wrong, and the child most certainly was. Come, let us do what we must and get it over with.'

I agreed that it should be I who should return to the mainland and seek the aid and advice of the local police.

Holmes gave me some last-minute instructions. 'I suggest that you try and inform them of the situation, Watson, without mention of your own strange part in the escapade or indeed of Miss Adler's. I will give the matter thought whilst you are gone and will decide just how much they need to know. I do not wish to conceal anything but then neither do I wish to confuse the issue. Do try and get hold of a detective rather than just a uniformed officer if you can, there's a good fellow.'

Gladly would I have swapped places with Holmes and allowed him the pleasure of making the first contact with the police, but I swallowed hard, grabbed my hat and set forth.

Once over the bridge I quickly located the nearest police station which was no more than half a mile along the main Salisbury road. I entered with some trepidation, wondering just where to begin.

The sergeant at the desk looked up at me wearily and enquired, 'Yes, squire, what can I be a doing of for you?'

'It's concerning the possible deaths of a woman and a newborn baby.'

He started a little but remained calm as he wrestled among a heap of official forms. Eventually he brought forth the one he presumably needed, took a pencil from behind his ear and licked its point.

'Your name, sir?'

'Watson, Dr John Watson.'

'Address?'

'221B Baker Street, London.'

'How about round here, are you staying locally or are you a tripper?'

'A tripper? Do I look like a tripper? I am staying at the inn, the Jolly Smugglers.'

'Oh yes, rum old place that, well named if you ask me.'

He tapped his nose in what I took to be a quite offensive manner.

'Sergeant, I don't know what you mean to imply. I am, for your information, staying there with an invalid friend who is in need of a break and a breath of sea air. We are not smugglers!'

'Right ho, sir, just my fun. Now what are the names of this woman and this newborn baby who you wish to report as dead? I take it the woman is not your wife or any close relative?'

'You are correct, though how you should know that I cannot see.'

'Why, sir, if it were your wife or sister you would be heartbroken and red about the eyes. I take it the child is not yours for the same reason. In fact I would say, judging from your manner, that this woman and child are not close to you at all.'

I wished that Holmes could have been with me, for I felt sure that this humble village police sergeant had an intellect rather shrouded by his station in life and seeming slowness of manner. I treated him with new respect.

'You are correct, Sergeant. In fact I have never set eyes on either of them to my knowledge. In the case of the newborn baby I can be certain that I have not.'

He ruminated for a few seconds, then evidently decided to start again from scratch. This came as a relief to me because I now felt that I had a few actual answers to his questions.

'Names, unknown then?'

'That is right!'

'Where then are these dead persons?'

'In the garden of a bungalow on Dolphin's Spine.'

'Are they recently deceased?'

'I have no idea.'

'Ah, they must be buried then, otherwise you as a medical man would have some idea through the decomposition or lack of it. Did you discover the places of interment yourself, sir?'

'Well, no, my friend believes them to be buried there.'

'This would be your invalid friend, so this whole matter is based upon an idea that your invalid friend has about some people buried in the garden?'

'Yes, he is all but certain.'

'This friend, he is not dippy is he, sir?'

'Certainly not, his name is Sherlock Holmes!'

'How long has he imagined himself to be Sherlock Holmes, sir?'

I realized that I would have to be a little more definite and convincing.

'Look here, Sergeant, you can tell that I am far from dippy as you so interestingly refer to a mental illness. Just take my word that my friend has very good reason to believe that there are bodies buried in the garden of a bungalow, *Mon Repos*. He is there with another friend, awaiting my return with a suitable officer, preferably a detective.'

'All right, sir, I'll take your word for it that this is not some potty wild-goose chase. I will accompany you there myself and if I am convinced that there is anything in it all, I will send for Inspector Cummings who is at Arundel, the nearest detective I know of.'

He called on a constable to take charge of the station and drove me himself in a police gig over the bridge to Dolphin's Spine. On the way I believe I managed to convince him that my friend was in fact the famous Baker Street investigator and that he was not about to meet some lunatic with delusions of identity.

# CHAPTER 5

# The Secret of *Mon Repos*

To my relief Holmes greeted the single police sergeant that I had produced with great courtesy. It was explained to him that the sergeant would need more evidence before sending to Arundel for Inspector Cummings.

'What is your name, sergeant?'

'Cooper, sir, and might I say that it is a great pleasure to meet you. I have long admired your methods of deduction and detection as chronicled by your friend, the doctor.'

'Splendid, Cooper, then let us investigate this little matter together.'

I would not myself have chosen the phrase 'little matter' to describe the possibility of two illicitly buried bodies, but Cooper did not pick up on that point. Instead he asked for a brief résumé of the events that had led up to the suspicions. Holmes did this briskly, leaving out entirely the reason for our visit to the locality, save that he had needed a rest, which was true enough.

'During the course of a visit to our friend, Miss Adler, we

discovered a woman's dress which was not Miss Adler's beneath a cushion. Alerted by the bloodstains I found a butcher's knife in the kitchen drawer which could have been an instrument involved in some kind of attack upon the wearer of the dress . . .'

Holmes went on to explain about the bloodstains under the table and something of his theory concerning the delivery, live birth, demise of the woman and later demise of the child after attempts had been made to save it. He showed the glove to Cooper who was bright enough to grasp the possibility of its use as a feeding medium for an infant. He had to have the possibility concerning the tracheotomy explained very carefully, but eventually grasped the significance of the bloodstained tear at the neck of the dress. He examined all the objects carefully and made copious notes. Then he closed his notebook and asked to see the suspected burial sites.

'You will notice, Sergeant Cooper, how the marine shrubs have not prospered in just two places.'

He understood the point. 'I think, Mr Holmes, that we should start with the smaller grave, or such as you believe it to be. After all, we might find some other logical reason for the plants being unhealthy? Doctor, if you would be so kind as to pass me the spade that you discovered, I will begin the gruesome task.'

He pushed the edge of the spade into the sandy shingle. I could scarcely describe it as soil. He lifted the roots of the plants and then started to dig away the stones, earth and sand. He did this with great care and eventually found something, and not more than about eighteen inches or so down. He paused and suggested that Miss Adler should absent herself from the scene, little knowing that she was made of stern stuff for a woman. When she protested that she did not wish to leave, he shrugged and continued to disinter that which he had found.

Dear reader, I am as you know, a medical man and used to seeing many a bizarre and gruesome sight. But that which was revealed was hardly either really, perhaps being best described as pathetic and heartrending. In a canvas wrapping there was the all but mummified body of a tiny child, little more than parchment skin over bones. As Holmes and I leaned forward to see it, we each raised a kerchief to our face.

Of course we were forbidden to touch the tiny, sad cadaver, with the sergeant informing us in choked tones that he would need to send at once for the police doctor and, of course, the famous Inspector Cummings. But I was able to examine, at least with my eyes, which told me something.

I explained to Holmes, 'The child is male, European, and was perhaps three days old at the time of death.'

'How long has he been dead, Watson. Can you tell at this stage?'

'At least two years, possibly rather more. I doubt if even the police doctor having taken the body into a laboratory will be able to be accurate beyond that. I think he will find it has been buried for a minimum of two years and not more than five. After that passage of time the skin would have started to peel from the bones.'

Cooper would not dig in the other suspected burial site.

He did not wish to take the responsibility for the discovery of the woman's body which we were now all certain lay beneath the longer row of faded marine shrubs.

The sergeant insisted that we all leave the scene of the crime as it could now actually be called, though as yet in the singular. This meant that Irene was without a roof over her head, and I remarked upon this fact. We conferred and decided that she could stay at the inn, the Jolly Smugglers. She agreed to this and quickly packed a few clothes and other necessities of life into a large suitcase.

Before we left for the inn, Holmes rather reluctantly surrendered his little collection of clues to Sergeant Cooper. Also we were delayed from leaving until Cooper had returned to his station and fetched from there a constable who could stand guard over *Mon Repos*.

Later that evening, Miss Adler, who had easily secured a room at the Jolly Smugglers, had joined us for dinner in the bar parlour. We had offered to look farther afield for a meal but Irene had insisted that our idea that a woman should not be seen in a public house was a little outdated.

'Gentlemen, were I to sit at one of those tables near the bar and start swilling pints of ale, I'll grant you heads might turn. But to sit here with the two of you to protect me, eating my dinner in what I hope is a ladylike manner, pray where is the harm?'

I was amazed how a diva could sit with two middle-aged gentlemen, eating a simple public house meal, followed by bread and cottage cheese and appear to be enjoying the experience. However, our enjoyment of the meal was soon to be interrupted by he whom Cooper had described as the famous Inspector Cummings. He was a huge man and in his tall hat was obliged to bow low as he entered the door of the apartment. He had a vast red face with grizzled mutton-chop whiskers. He saw Irene and removed his hat to reveal a full head of greying hair.

He spoke with a normally booming voice which he seemed to be lowering so that he took on a truly conspiratorial tone. 'Which of you is Sherlock Holmes?'

My friend answered, 'I am he, the very same. Whom have I the pleasure to address?'

'Inspector Cummings, and I believe you have been meddling in affairs that do not concern you?'

Sherlock Holmes lit an Egyptian cigarette before he replied. 'Inspector, it is every citizen's duty to report to the police any trace of wrongdoing that he might suspect. Had I alerted your local sergeant any earlier you and he would surely have accused me of wasting your time. I had to be reasonably sure that a crime had been committed before I spoke up!'

'Well, be that as it may, despite the report of the sergeant, I fail to see why you were drawn into this affair in the first place. It is a bit far from Baker Street, is it not?'

At this point I sighed deeply, knowing that we would have to tell the whole story, but first I enquired, 'You have found the woman's body, buried where we suspected it might be?'

'Yes we have, and the police doctor is examining it, along with that poor child's body at this moment. But I was addressing Sherlock Holmes.'

For the ensuing fifteen minutes Holmes explained the whole story to Cummings: his illness, the concern of Mycroft and Irene, their kindly laying of clues to be conveyed by myself, our journey to Dolphin's Spine and our discovery that Mr and Mrs Reiner were one and the same, finally the examination of the dress, knife and kitchen table.

Holmes laid all his cards upon the table and the more he spoke the more the inspector's wonder seemed to grow. 'Dr Watson, Miss Adler, do you both confirm what Holmes has said?'

We both nodded and expressed our agreement with Holmes's version of the happenings of the few days past. But I could see that he was not entirely convinced.

'I know, Holmes, that you are renowned for deduction, but to have discovered all of this which your friends purport to have been a form of hoax, and for you then to find a real crime when investigating it seems more than a trifle far-fetched! I will tell you this, all three of you, I am going to get in touch with this so-called brother Mycroft, and if he does not exist or have the powers which you suggest, I will arrest all three of you. For the moment you are to remain in the close vicinity of this inn. Cooper will be keeping an eye on you, and if I do not find other logical suspects quickly, you will certainly be seeing me again, and soon. Goodnight to you!'

He nodded curtly and left the bar parlour, leaving us to consider this turn of events.

I was the first to speak. 'I wonder if they found the throat wound on the woman's body, Holmes?'

'Oh I feel sure they have, for had they not he would have picked up upon that point with gleeful triumph. Inspector

Cummings is not a particularly pleasant man, but I have no doubt his medical condition worsens his temper. Come, Watson, you of all people must have suspected his maladies?'

'You mean his athlete's foot?'

'Good man, you did notice the way he kept attacking one boot with the toe of the other. It is the wrong time of year for chilblains.'

Irene cut in brightly, her wonderful eyes opened wide. 'And even I recognized his glandular condition, though for the life of me I cannot give it a name.'

'Gigantism . . .' (I felt best qualified to speak) 'a condition of the glands which causes the skeleton to be larger than normal. Typical symptom is a very prominent jaw, apart from the obvious one, extremity of size.'

Holmes grunted, lit yet another Egyptian cigarette and said, 'Good old Watson, you can always be relied upon to provide a technical answer to explain the obvious. Shall we just say that he is a very large man, extremely un-pleasant and in my view not overburdened with intellect. Fortunately we will not be followed about by him in person when we wish to leave the inn upon some errand or other.'

'You make very light of the fact that we could all be arrested' (Irene expressed what was in my mind), 'if not for murder at least for complicity or the concealment of evidence. Gentlemen, I have got you into this, at least Mycroft and I have got you into it. But seeing our dear Sherlock so well and alert makes it all worth while.'

'My dear Miss Adler, you consider I would be better off a bright and alert convict than a vegetable at liberty. Do not fret, dear lady, your actions were well meant and even greatly appreciated by me in my own quiet way. But above all, the police should really be grateful to you for bringing the whole matter to their attention. As for our plight, please do not worry, Mycroft will put Cummings in his place. Or, if not, we have only to solve the mystery to prove ourselves innocent of involvement.'

It was not until about eleven of the clock that any of us ventured forth upon the following morning. It was decided that I should be delegated to visit the newsagent and the tobacconist to see what effect this might have on our police supervision. As I left the inn I noticed a figure in a tweed suit and billycock hat standing by the bridge. He showed great interest in my movements but tried to appear uninterested; he was a very bad actor. This was especially obvious when he started to follow me, walking with a strolling gait and whistling as if completely indifferent to my movements. I entered the newsagent's shop and purchased *The Times* and a somewhat lighter broadsheet for Miss Adler. When I emerged, the fellow had shown the good sense to stroll on a little further, allowing me to catch him up. I passed him just before we reached the tobacconist and touched my hat and bade him good morning!

The tobacconist was a cheerful soul and passed the time of day with me as he weighed a few ounces of Scottish mixture on his scale. As I paid for this, two or three cigars and a package of twenty Pasha, I confided in him.

'There is someone outside whom I wish to avoid. Do you

think I could emerge through the back entrance to your shop?'

'Is it the police?'

'Yes.'

'Are you a thief or a murderer?'

'No.'

'A dangerous lunatic or an anarchist?'

'Gracious no!'

'You are not . . .' (he lowered his voice) 'a freemason or anything like that?'

I assured him that I was not and he grinned and beckoned to me to follow him. He led me through his parlour where a lady, probably his wife, looked up from her knitting and smiled at me.

He introduced us as we moved onward toward his back door. 'This gentleman is just going out the back way to avoid the police, Molly. Don't worry, he's not a mason.'

'Oh, right ho then!' She waved and smiled, then returned to her knitting as if fugitives were an everyday occurrence! We emerged into a sort of back double and he pointed, saying, 'A few steps that way will take you out into the lane which will take you to the inn if you turn left and to the railway if you turn right.'

I thanked him profusely and decided to walk up toward the station to see if I had lost my shadow.

This appeared to be so, and I decided to stroll until I reached the railway and then stroll back to the inn to see what would happen. But as I strolled I was suddenly addressed by a familiar voice. It belonged to the driver of the dilapidated cab.

'What ho, Doctor! I'm glad to see you again, old Captain likewise. How are you and your pal gettin' on at the Jolly Smugglers?'

He insisted that I climb into the vehicle. I decided not to tell Murray too much, save that I was trying to elude the attentions of a plainclothes policeman. His eyes widened at this news, but undismayed he bade me don an old coat and hat which he produced from a compartment beneath the vehicle.

'Put those on, guv', and he will never recognize you, especially in a cab. Shove your own duds under the seat and change back when we gets there.'

As if in a trance I obeyed, and the reader can believe me when I say that when we passed the bewildered man in the tweed suit, he scarcely gave us a second glance, being far too busy looking for the John Watson that had entered the tobacconist's and failed to emerge. It would hardly have been his game to enter the shop in his search for me, wishing to be as little noticed as possible.

'My dear Watson, where have you been? We have been waiting altogether too long for the papers and the tobacco. Do you know I was about to send Miss Adler to look for you!'

Sherlock Holmes was touchy, but it was only due to his having run out of the Scottish mixture. As it was he was smoking a Russian cigarette of the kind that is wedged into a cardboard tube. He cast it aside, muttering, 'Miss Adler had nothing better . . .' He transferred the shredded tobacco leaves into his pouch with frenzied fingers, very swiftly placing some in turn into the bowl of his pipe. 'No wonder the Russians are so strange of temper, Watson, if they smoke such foul tobacco in such a strange manner.' He lit his vesta and the heavenly blue cloud calmed him.

We sat in the bar parlour and I told him of my adventures.

'Upon my word, Watson, it falls out that you are more than suited to the role of a fugitive from justice. What is more, you have a special talent for recruiting aides as disgraceful as yourself. I feel sure that the tobacconist would not have helped me to escape from my shadower, and if your friend the cab driver had not known you in Afghanistan he would scarce have given me a second look let alone drive me, heavily disguised, through the streets.'

His irony was beginning to irritate me and I was glad when Irene came onto the scene to provide a distraction. She was radiant in green velour. I remarked upon the grace which she lent the gown but Holmes just grunted, though I felt sure it was being worn for his benefit. Life is cruel really, for here was I, a widower who found her so adorable, yet she only had eyes for Sherlock Holmes who would never do more than respect and admire her.

He made me repeat my story of my morning's activities and Irene clapped her hands and laughed merrily. 'Oh John, you really are a scream, and where do you imagine your follower to be now?'

But my reply was cut short by the entrance of Inspector Cummings. He appeared to be in a fury of a temper which he seemed to find it diplomatic to control.

'Your brother, Mycroft, really is the big man with the

government, not to speak of Scotland Yard! I was actually admonished for my so-called dismissive treatment of you. Well, I am supposed to let you aid me in any way you can, though I cannot see how you can find any facts that I am not capable of discovering. So, I must allow you to assist, but I do so, sir, with bad grace, very bad grace indeed. Well, what do you wish to do now?'

'Pray calm yourself, Inspector, for at present I wish to finish a pipe which I am smoking and a pint of ale which I have before me. Whilst I do so I suggest that you tell me of your latest findings.'

'My plainclothes detective shadowed your friend and lost him. Then the wire from Scotland Yard made me withdraw him anyway. The exhumed body of a young woman has been taken to the mortuary, and you are welcome to inspect it if you have the stomach for such things.'

Holmes rather surprised me when he failed to take advantage of the inspector's offer. But as ever there was wisdom in his words.

'I am not squeamish, Inspector, and Watson is a doctor. But there is little point in our inspecting that which is what we would expect to find. Did you, for instance, locate the throat wound which was inflicted solely to aid her breathing?'

'Why yes, and the police doctor discovered that she had given birth at about the time of her death, which probably occurred about three years ago. She was naked and wrapped in sacking, fair haired, about five and twenty, in roughly the same state of decomposition as the infant.'

I wondered at Holmes allowing this conversation in

front of Irene and without warning. As so often he appeared to read my thoughts, turning to me and saying, 'Watson, you do Miss Adler a disservice if you consider that she should have been sent from the room like a child whilst the adults discuss unsuitable topics!'

I was badly hurt, but she touched my hand and spoke to me gently. 'My dear John, I am grateful for your consideration for me, but I am a woman of the world. I have heard things that were so much worse to listen to. Forgive your friend, he is at times unworthy of you.'

She glared at Holmes who spoke more gently. 'Watson, Miss Adler is right, right that I knew she would be undismayed, but also right in her feeling that my treatment of my only friend is unworthy. Please forgive me. Now, Inspector, have you any sort of clues of which I am unaware and which we might follow?'

Cummings was as unbearable as ever in his manner. 'Oh, I feel sure that you can produce a rabbit of a clue from a top hat of a situation. I'll give you the pleasure of making the next move.'

'Inspector, I suggest that we visit the agent who lets the bungalow to those who wish to reside at *Mon Repos*. His name is Scrooby and his style is Scrooby & Co. and we had some contact with him a day or so ago. We asked him something of the letting history of the bungalow, but at that time we were unsure of the period that was of main interest to us. Doubtless he has some records which you have the power to force him to show you.'

Cummings lifted his hat and placing it upon his head became once more a virtual seven feet tall. He grunted and beckoned us to follow him. We made quite a parade, Cummings, Holmes, myself, Irene and the sergeant.

Is it not strange how the most unlikely thought enters one's head at the most inexplicable moment of time? As we walked I not only had such a random thought, but I actually voiced it. 'Funny, I could have sworn that Captain was a grey!'

Holmes looked at me with, for himself, strange tolerance, appearing to know exactly about that to which I referred.

'Time can play its tricks, Watson, but hold on to that thought in case it should fall into its rightful place in the future.'

The thought of course had been connected with Murray and Captain, the horse that had evidently played its part in saving my life. I was glad that he had managed to avoid the knacker's yard and to be likely to spend the rest of his days in the lightest of work and excellent care. Yet . . . I still could not rid myself of this vision of myself lying across the back of a grey.

Scrooby was not exactly delighted to see us I felt. His eyes fixed first upon Holmes and myself and their light registered recognition and lack of any great interest. As he caught sight of Irene he managed a faint smile which faded as soon as the huge inspector lowered his head in order to pass through the door frame. I suspected that Scrooby had never clapped eyes upon Cummings before, yet instantly knew him for a policeman.

The letting agent proved to have a retentive memory as he greeted us, if as a greeting his crusty words could be described.

'Mr Reynolds, Dr Snipe and Mrs Reiner, is it not?'

Then he glanced questioningly at Cummings who introduced himself.

'Mr Scrooby, I am Inspector Cummings of the Arundel detective force, out of my regular area through force of circumstance and the illness of a colleague. These gentlemen are in fact Sherlock Holmes and Dr Watson' (his voice took on a sarcastic tone), 'the famous sleuths!'

I was far from delighted that he had elected to make us seem foolish; however, to his credit, Scrooby spared us further grief. 'Just so, false names to aid detective efforts? Very understandable, gentlemen. I presume Mrs Reiner is still Mrs Reiner?'

It was his turn to trot out the sarcasm. Irene coloured slightly. I tried to save her any further embarrassment with my next words. 'The lady you have known as Mrs Reiner is in fact Miss Irene Adler, the celebrated opera singer. She is helping us with our enquiries.'

I could not help but feel that I was making matters worse!

Scrooby looked thoughtful and asked Irene a pointed question. 'Miss Adler, when I let *Mon Repos* to you, were you and your husband already engaged in, how shall I put it, an investigation?'

'I will have to draw a veil over the subject, Mr Scrooby, until I know what Inspector Cummings will allow me to discuss.'

A masterpiece of diplomacy I reckoned, especially with the unfortunate question concerning the whereabouts of Dale Reiner obviously on the tip of Scrooby's tongue.

Cummings at this point brought up the subject of the past residents of *Mon Repos*. He also asked if there was any kind of a list of such persons that we might inspect. We were shown a form of rental book. Cumming's finger ran down the list of names.

He said, 'Here is the area of our search, 1894 and 1895. You will notice, Holmes, that one name is shown as occupant from March '94 until the November of '95. The name is Arkwright, and the initial appears to be a W. What do you know to tell us concerning a W. Arkwright, Mr Scrooby?'

'A good tenant, always paid his rent on time. I was sorry when he had to leave to join his ailing mother in Manchester.'

'Do you have a forwarding address?'

'I had, but I have no record of it any more.'

Holmes was still glancing at the rent book with interest but made no comment. Cummings nodded to Scrooby and made for the door, saying over his shoulder, 'You have been most helpful, Mr Scrooby. We will trouble you no more for the moment. There may be more that I need to talk to you about. We are investigating a possible murder.'

As he left the office Irene said to Scrooby words to the effect that she wished to terminate her rental of *Mon Repos*. 'I will call and make final settlement later in the week. I will be leaving on Monday.'

Once outside the building, Cummings asked Holmes concerning his next intended move. When Sherlock hesitated in order to charge his clay, the inspector became impatient of manner and snapped out his words.

'Mr Holmes, I do not have all day to await your reply. I intend to return to Arundel, thereafter to take the train to

Manchester where I consider my best field of investigation lies. You may do as you please, but remember you are yourselves implicated to some extent and must inform the local police if you wish to leave the area. Be sure to leave your intended destination should you decide to vacate the inn.'

He touched his hat to Miss Adler and turned on his heel and was away like a villain in a melodrama making an exit. The sergeant winked at us as they left.

Sherlock Holmes lit his pipe carefully and drew the acrid smoke into his long-polluted lungs. Then he expelled it, smiled enigmatically and spoke.

'My dear Watson, Miss Adler . . . it promises to be an extremely pleasant day despite the strong breeze.'

That evening we decided to accompany Irene to *Mon Repos* in order that we might help her in the collection of her remaining possessions, those left through our somewhat hurried earlier departure. We reckoned that there had been time enough for the authorities to have ended any search and would be less touchy concerning our presence. This proved to be so, for we found Sergeant Cooper in sole charge of the bungalow, and inclined to let us have a free rein.

'We have been all over everything and turned up nothing of interest. We thought we were onto something when we found a false moustache, but then I remembered that, alas, this Miss Adler has already revealed to us.'

We all chuckled at this, especially Irene. Cooper continued, 'You can go inside now, Miss, and collect whatever is yours. I am just here to make sure that there are no intruders. Not much in there to intrude upon though, is there?'

As soon as we were inside and unobserved, Holmes busied himself. Whilst Irene packed her things into a suitcase, he stalked around peering behind articles of furniture.

'You would be amazed at what can turn up behind a sideboard or a dresser. Moreover, these are the last places where the police think to look. The man who interests us left quickly so who knows what he may have overlooked.'

Just when it seemed as if his search would be fruitless, Holmes beckoned to me to aid him in the movement of a small bookcase. It was deceptively heavy despite its compact size. Had there been books upon its shelves, which there were not, we would doubtless have been forced to remove them before moving the object. As we moved the piece forward there was the unmistakable sharp sound of an object falling behind it. This proved to be a thick cardboard panel of the economy variety, much used by artists who have more talent than money.

Holmes held up the panel and removing its dusty covering with his handkerchief he revealed a splendid portrait of an attractive young woman in a voluminous dress with leg of mutton sleeves. She was depicted smiling, to reveal uneven teeth which gave character to her face.

There was excitement in the detective's voice as he spoke, 'Watson, Miss Adler, you see *Mon Repos* has indeed offered up one of its more important secrets!'

# CHAPTER 6

# The Picture Tells Its Story

'Upon my word, Holmes, is that not the dress with the bloodstains and the knife slit?'

But he shook his head at my words. 'No, Watson, for if you look carefully you will see that its colour and style are rather different. It is the style with those outdated sleeves which is the point of likeness.'

'Perhaps it was painted a decade ago?'

Again he shook his head, 'The paint, which is oil based, is dry enough for the painting to have been executed a few years ago, but the drying process is extremely slow, though not as slow as that. Ten years would have made it bone dry.'

He illustrated his point by flaking some soft paint from the corner of the board with his thumbnail.

'You see? No, it is a case of the subject favouring that fashion which other women had long abandoned. She is young, she is pleasing of appearance and one is tempted to believe that she wore the sleeves to perhaps hide some disfigurement. A scar or birthmark on one of her arms.'

We decided to take the painting with us, it being small enough to lay in Irene's suitcase beneath her clothing.

Back at the inn, to which we quickly returned having found no other useful clues, we propped the painting upon a chair in Holmes's bedroom where we congregated.

'It is a very fine painting, is it not?'

This was all that I could think to add to that which Holmes had already discovered. Irene could only add that the lady was very attractive. But Holmes had not as yet finished with his job of extracting the final globule of factual juice.

'It was indeed painted at *Mon Repos*, not inside but in the garden. Do you observe, Watson, the tiny depiction of a lighthouse which appears, all but on the horizon?'

'Can you be sure, Holmes, that it is the same lighthouse as the one which can be seen on a clear day from *Mon Repos*?'

But he handed me his lens without spoken reply. I peered through it at the painted structure and had to agree that its details matched.

'Unfortunately the portrait is not signed, so the artist will be more difficult to identify than the model.'

'Do you believe that the remains will offer any means of comparison?'

'Oh yes, if her teeth are slightly crooked I will be convinced that the body is that of this woman, even if there are no scars upon the arms.'

On the day following, Holmes contacted Sergeant Cooper and requested that he and I might after all be allowed to examine the cadaver of the woman.

He was not happy, but said, 'Well, I remember Inspector Cummings giving you a more or less free hand to investigate. But Mr Holmes, she is not a pleasant sight, and I cannot allow Miss Adler to go with us to the mortuary.'

Holmes assured him that he had no intention of allowing Irene to endure such an ordeal. Moreover he suggested that Cooper need not even enter the building himself if he did not wish to. This worked wonders and I realized that Cooper was that rarity, a sensitive policeman.

Unless you have experienced it, you can, dear reader, have little idea of what it is like to be forced to examine human remains that have been in the ground for a number of years, without even the refinement of a sarcophagus. As the sheet was pulled back I knew from experience what to expect and from our recent converse what to look for. I noticed first a badly mended fracture of the right upper arm, making the bone and, of course, that limb crooked. Then I investigated the top teeth, still intact but indeed somewhat crooked.

I looked at Holmes and nodded my agreement, then said, 'This is indeed the young woman in the portrait.'

Outside the mortuary we both hastily lit our pipes and smoked in silence for a minute or two. We could not tell Cooper of our findings because we would have had to reveal our concealment of the discovery of the portrait. After we had left him I turned to Holmes and enquired, 'Do you think we should continue to sit upon the painting. Perhaps it would, along with our findings, aid Cummings in his investigation?'

'That clodhopper?' (Holmes seemed livid at the very thought of Cummings.) 'Why he would frighten off and be unable to capture a tortoise! No, we have to go softly if we are to find our man. After all, we are still not sure that we are dealing with that which is a criminal act, save to the letter of the law.'

When Cummings returned from Manchester he was a little put out to hear of our visit to the mortuary. However, he had been ordered by his superiors to cooperate with us. He sniffed and asked if we had discovered anything. We said that we had not but that all avenues needed to be explored.

Then he revealed his real unpleasant depth of character when he said, 'You had the chance to go with me to the mortuary but you turned it down. Yet you decided to go on in without anyone else. What was the matter, were you scared that you might show yourselves up by fainting, or retching, or even blubbering?'

Sherlock Holmes rose to his feet and fixed the inspector with his gimlet eyes. He held the pose and the policeman's gaze for quite a few seconds before he spoke.

'Inspector Cummings, you will be good enough to treat my colleague who is a seasoned medical man, and a veteran of the Afghan campaign where he saved many lives and was forced to witness sights which would make you delirious with horror, with respect. As for myself, your opinions and feelings toward me are immaterial. Watson will tell you that I am a cold fish and care little what others think of me. As for my opinion concerning yourself, I have none. I find you to be just an irritant and a minor nuisance.'

I had never heard Holmes speak to any living soul in such a way before. I could see that he was furious, and but for his superb self-control would doubtless have landed us with problems of a violent nature. As it was, he just turned on his heel and made to leave.

But as we started back for the inn, Cummings called after Holmes in a manner most unbecoming for a public servant of high rank: 'I don't want you meddling in my professional investigations, Holmes. Carry out your own enquiries but be warned to stay within the law. We will see who solves this case!'

Holmes inclined his head a fraction and said, 'That it is solved is important, but just who claims the solution is unimportant. I wish you good evening . . .'

Over yet another unpretentious but sustaining dinner at the Jolly Smugglers, we brought Irene up to date upon our findings. Then Holmes suggested that we should return to Baker Street upon the morrow.

'I believe we have learned all that we can here. There are thoughts in my mind concerning my next moves, and they will take me to places far from here though not too far from Baker Street. Miss Adler, I cannot suggest that you stay with us at 221B, for obvious reasons, but there is a small private hotel almost opposite where you could stay. I often put up clients there and it is a safe and respectable house.'

She smiled with radiance, but said, 'Perhaps in a week or two. Meanwhile I shall stay here at the inn, my residence at *Mon Repos* being now terminated by circumstance. I would rather like a few more days here, and can of course keep my eyes open for any uncollected scraps that the great Sherlock Holmes may have missed.'

Holmes chuckled and said, 'I am sure there are many, my dear Miss Adler. In fact I feel sure that my past life and career has left an endless number of untidy ends.'

She looked at him, 'My dear Sherlock, do you not sometimes wish that you could have your time over again?'

'Frequently, Miss Adler, yet I doubt if I would want it to have been any different, for had I not followed my present calling many people would now be either demised or living in circumstances most unfortunate. I list among them persons from the highest and lowest levels of society, including Her Majesty the Queen.'

I hastily filled our glasses and we toasted the Monarch. Irene joined in with a certain lack of enthusiasm, then saying, 'John, your friend is not always as gallant as I would wish!'

Our return by train to London was singularly uneventful and Holmes was very uncommunicative concerning his immediate plans. I have learned from long experience never to place pressure upon him at such times. When Holmes wishes me to know something he will inform me of it in his own good time. But there was one incident which occurred at Brighton Station which is worthy of mention. We were in the waiting room, and a ten-year-old boy sat with his mother and small sister, opposite to ourselves. Most healthy minded British boys of course yearn to be soldiers or sailors and tend to wear clothes and favours such as suits with sailors' collars, or the wearing of paper hats in a military style. But this child, earnest of expression, was wearing a deerstalker cap, and holding a large magnifying lens. In his freehand he clutched a back issue of *The Strand* magazine, in which one of my accounts of a past case concerning my friend had appeared.

After having cavorted about, to be sure that all eyes were upon him and all ears ready to hear his words, he said, 'Elementary, Winifred, your chocolate creams were on the seat and now they are not, but I feel sure that I can deduce what has happened to them. If you want me to take your case, you will have to give me one of your jelly babies. I never vary my fee except where I lets 'em off altogether!'

As we climbed upon the Victoria-bound train, Holmes muttered to me, 'My dear Watson, what have you done? To make the whole thing worse, the child had himself stolen his sister's sweets, as traces of chocolate cream upon his mouth betrayed!'

Mrs Hudson was delighted to see us and greeted Sherlock Holmes with great warmth.

'Mr Holmes, welcome back, and may I say how wonderful it is to see you looking just like your old self again! Why when you left here you were still looking a bit peaky, but I can see that a dose of sea air has done the trick.'

I muttered to Holmes, under my breath, 'That and a couple of decomposed bodies!'

The good lady, forewarned by our wire, had prepared a really splendid meal. There was a game pie that any gourmet would have killed for and a splendid pudding in the form of an ice bomb with hot chocolate sauce, a masterpiece of timing for the hot and cold elements. But it was not until we lingered over coffee and liqueurs that Holmes mellowed enough to give me even a hint of his future plans.

'What, Watson, is your opinion of the painting which we discovered at *Mon Repos*?'

I tried to make my reply objective. 'Well, it is an excellent portrait, and I doubt if it is the work of a tyro or student.'

'Exactly. In fact I would go so far as to say that it is a quite important work of art and whoever painted it has either gone on to fame and fortune or is an undiscovered genius.'

'This being so, then it might be easy enough to discover him?'

'Possibly. This very evening I will consult a friend who deals in works of art. But that it was not signed is a great pity.'

Geoffrey Malpasse examined the painting with great care, both at close quarters and from a distance having placed it upon an easel. He looked at it wearing his gold-rimmed pince-nez and he looked at it without their aid.

Finally he turned to us and said, 'My dear Holmes, I cannot tell you who painted this portrait but I can say something of its quality. As an agent for a great many leading artists, my humble opinion is that I have seldom seen such a striking and vibrant portrait. Why, it is almost as if the young lady could move and speak and something of his technique makes you feel as if you know her as a friend. I tell you this, Holmes, if you can bring this man to me I can get him a dozen patrons if he is willing to paint the great and the famous. I say "if" because artists are a strange crowd. Some of them will refuse such commissions, stating that they paint only who and what they desire to. Well, well, that's all very well but it does not pay the bills. It is possible that our friend here is still completely undiscovered. I for one have never encountered his work before, or I would at once have recognized his style. That is what the picture has, style . . . and brilliance.'

'So I might find him in some attic studio in Chelsea or Camden?'

'Quite possibly, if he is not the kind who would wish to work in Paris. One can live cheaply there, but certainly Chelsea is as good a bet as any.'

I don't know what I imagined would be Holmes's next move. I suppose I thought that he would perhaps go to Chelsea and make a few enquiries. But I was ill-prepared for the elaborate plans that he was considering.

On the following morning I arose at a somewhat late hour, revelling in the comfort of my own bed again. Imagine my surprise to find a strange, rather unkempt individual sitting in Holmes's chair at the breakfast table and fast demolishing his bacon and mushrooms.

I must have started before I spoke, 'Upon my word, sir, you have the advantage of me. Are you a client of my friend, Mr Sherlock Holmes?'

He rubbed a slice of bread in the fat upon his plate and scratched his long matted hair with his fork. He had a scruffy chin, though this brown stubble could scarce be called a beard. His nose was veined as if through the misuse of alcohol. When he spoke it was with a husky voice, though not an entirely uncultured one in its tone. His eyes peered at me through thick-lensed spectacles which were minus one side support, giving his face a strangely comical lopsided look.

'Client? No, I'm not a client, sir, I am more like an expert. You see I am an artist and I have promised to look at a portrait for Mr Holmes. I understand he is anxious to identify the sitter and the artist. Well, nobody better than me for a job like that. I know them all, artists and models alike.'

Beginning to understand the reason for his presence, I was yet slightly suspicious. 'Did anyone give you permission to eat that breakfast?'

'Permission? No, some old girl showed me in here and it was on the table. I assumed it was meant for me so I piled in, sir!'

'I believe that breakfast was meant for Sherlock Holmes!'

'Oh yes, well it's a bit late to tell me that now.'

Mrs Hudson entered with my breakfast which she placed before me. She looked at the scruffy one and cast her eyes heavenwards for my benefit as she passed me on her way out of the room. I took this to mean that although she did not approve she had received orders to accept this strange presence. I remember wishing that Holmes would put in an appearance to deal with his expert himself. Eventually I rose and tapped upon his bedroom door, calling to him to the effect that his visitor was waiting. After I repeated this knocking and calling, to my relief I heard Holmes's voice, but I was startled that it seemed to come from behind me rather than from his room.

'My dear Watson, I am delighted that my disguise is such a success!'

I wheeled around to face again the bohemian and realize not for the first time that my friend was a past master in theatrical transformation. Though perhaps I should qualify that because where an actor like Sir Henry Irving might sit at the table in heavy character alteration and make it impossible for one to recognize him, one would still be aware of the presence of thespian cosmetics applied to his features. Holmes had discovered the art of being able to apply it so sparingly yet tellingly that one did not suspect its presence, even without the air of footlights or flood lamps.

I rounded upon him. 'Really, Holmes, must you play your schoolboy pranks upon me so early in the morning?'

'My dear fellow, I never play pranks, even upon yourself.'

'Then why this charade?'

'If you mean why did I try out my disguise upon my best, nay only, friend? Well, the answer is obvious: that if it would work upon you it would be safe to assume that I could move abroad thus disguised without fear of being recognized. But your question obviously also concerns the deeper purpose of my deception. I wish to be taken for a working artist, trying to sell his latest painting. I am going to take the picture that we discovered at *Mon Repos*, and I am going to show it to people in the artistic world, in the hope that the style might pull a string upon someone's memory.'

'But, Holmes, suppose the real artist should discover you, trying to pass his picture off as yours?'

Sherlock Holmes slapped at his bewigged pate with his right palm, gasping rather than speaking.

'Watson, you amaze me! Does it not occur to you that this is the very scenario that I wish to bring about? If I were to merely show the picture around, the painter of it might think twice before speaking up. But what artistic spirit could bear the sight and sound of some bogus painter claiming to have produced his work? You will also have your part to play in our little drama, Watson, but after your recent remark I can see that I will have to explain it rather more carefully than I might have thought necessary. You will play the part of a man of means, interested in the purchase of works of art. Our bargaining and haggling may, I believe, draw interest from those with information which might be impossible to collect in any other way.'

'But, Holmes,' I protested, 'you could publish a likeness of the painting in some journal and it would be seen by a great many more people, would it not?'

Holmes all but lost his temper with me but checked himself in good time. 'The presentation of the reproduction would be rather like a police notice of the "have you seen this person" type. My little drama is designed to make the rightfully astonished artist, or someone close to him, unable to keep his peace.'

I was not entirely convinced of the sagacity of his plan, but of course I decided to go along with Holmes and help him in any way.

'Do you wish me to also adopt a disguise?'

'Certainly not, Watson; your personna is not as well known as mine, and you can thank your illustrator Sydney Paget for that. He usually depicts you as being even more respectable and every day that is indeed the case. All I ask is that you take your theatrical cue from me. Come, we will away to Chelsea, which I have chosen as a likely jumping-off area for our little deception. One of the public houses in the Kings Road, much frequented by artists, would be as good a place as any to begin.'

Half an hour later we stood in Baker Street, I in my regular style of attire and Holmes in his artistic disguise, complete with paintbox and portfolio. From habit I let the first two hansom cabs pass us by. This presented no difficulty, for their drivers did not linger when they saw my companion. The third driver stopped for us, but did so rather tentatively, if one can so do with a horse and vehicle. But at least that was the impression I received. As it fell out, the driver was known to us and as we climbed in and I bade him take us to the Kings Road, Chelsea, he nodded, touched his hat and bent over to speak quietly to me.

'Take care, Dr Watson, you've got a dodgy customer here. I'd be more at ease if Mr Holmes were with you!'

I changed a chuckle into a cough and replied with equally muted voice, 'Don't worry, Hawkins, he is not far away!'

Of course, Holmes's acute hearing picked up my words and although he made no comment he breathed hard, as if to say, 'Watch your words, Watson.'

The cabby made a direct route for Victoria and then made a turn to the right toward Sloane Square. When we reached that fashionable quadrant, he leaned down and asked, 'Where exactly in the Kings Road, Doctor?'

I looked enquiringly at Holmes, who said, 'The Lord Nelson!'

Within a few minutes the cab had stopped outside that

hostelry and we had stepped down onto the pavement of one of London's most interesting and bohemian of thoroughfares. We entered the public bar which was thronged with imbibers, most of them rather artistic in appearance. Holmes began to revel in his role as a downtrodden genius. He placed the painting on the bench seat and bade me sit beside it whilst he made for the bar. By the time he returned with two tankards of ale it had attracted quite an amount of attention.

I should mention that ours was by no means the only painting thus displayed, and I realized that the worldly Holmes had selected this particular hostelry from his knowledge of its style. Surely the perfect place for our enactment to begin.

'Five pounds you say, a fiver for a masterpiece? Why if you were not sitting there all dressed up like a dog's dinner I would say that you were no gentleman!'

I picked up my cue in the reply. 'I have no wish to insult your work, sir, which is excellent. But you are not a known painter, at least not to me. Why you have not even signed the painting!'

We carried on with variations on this theme for a few minutes until Holmes made as if to open his paints in order to sign the painting. But to my amazement, a roughly dressed bearded fellow interrupted.

'Hey, just a minute, you can't sign that for it is not your work.'

'Who says so, who says it is not my work? Not my work?' Holmes expostulated. 'Whose work is it then if it is not mine?'

'I don't know his name, but I've seen him around, sometimes painting the boats at the embankment. The style is unmistakable. He drinks in the Eight Bells and Bowling Green, practically opposite. I'll wager you won't take it in there and sign it, in a place where his work is known.'

Holmes rose, and picked up the painting and the art box and with a derisive gesture he left the bar. I did not at once follow him, feeling that this might seem suspicious. After all, as a patron of the arts I would perhaps have had my interest in the painting somewhat reduced by this little scene. Other artists thrust paintings at me and I examined several of them in a manner which I felt to be a convincing one. Eventually I took the opportunity to depart.

Outside I glanced around for the Eight Bells and Bowling Green, finding it easily by the eight bells hanging outside its edifice. I entered its public bar to find Holmes already hard at work in trying to interest fellow drinkers in the painting. I took up my character again and tried to bargain for the picture. Keeping my eyes and ears open I noticed a short, bearded man wearing corduroy trousers and sabots. His jacket was, of course, linen and he carried a broad panama hat. I say I noticed him because although he left the immediate vicinity of Holmes and the painting from time to time he, unlike most others, ever returned to the spot. Of course, I assumed that Holmes had noticed him and later I would know that this was indeed so.

After a while I began to run out of different ways of handling my pretended negotiations with Holmes the artist. So I was glad when he suddenly seemed to have a fresh thought upon it himself. He fished a scrap of paper and a stub of pencil from his pocket and, scrawling on the paper, spoke warmly.

'Very well, sir, I see we are getting nowhere. I will write an amount upon this paper, the lowest I will accept for the picture. Then you can either accept it or not as you wish. If you do not, it is my final word and I will hear no more from you.'

He passed me the paper, folded. I opened it and peered at the message which I made sure that only I could read. It said, 'Make a scene that will empty the bar and rush out into the street yourself.'

I was confronted with a monumental task of histrionics. I like to think that I excelled myself as I clutched at the side of my jacket and shouted, 'My wallet has been taken . . . quick there he goes . . . a sovereign for whoever catches the thief!'

I pointed toward the entrance door and then made toward it myself. Within half a minute I estimated that almost everyone who had been in the bar had joined me in the street including Sherlock Holmes.

He whispered to me, urgently, 'Watch for someone emerging from the building, clutching the painting!'

Alas no such figure emerged, although the suspicious character did himself appear but certainly not clutching the painting. He wandered off in the direction of the Worlds End. Gradually we filtered back into the public bar and I saw, as did Holmes, that the painting was still in its position, propped against the back of a sofa. I thought it diplomatic to make a retreat at this point lest someone accused me of creating alarm and panic. I could in fact see the proprietor of the establishment making toward me. I took a cab to Baker Street, considering that I had played my part well enough for one day.

I had been back at the rooms for about an hour and a half when Holmes arrived, still in his disguise and carrying his art box and the painting. These he put down upon the table and, grunting, he retreated to his bedroom. I felt it wise to say nothing, for with his plans having produced evidently no result his mood might be better deferred than savoured. However, when he emerged, wearing his faded pink dressing gown and minus his disguise his manner was rather more jaunty than I might have expected it to be.

'Well, Watson, I see you decided that discretion was indeed the better part of valour. Very wise to retreat when there is little else that one can do. Are there any crumpets for tea by the way?'

It was not until he was enjoying his buttered crumpets and seemed of mellow mood that I dared to again raise the matter of the painting.

'What a pity it all came to nothing, after all the trouble you took with the disguise and everything, but at least I avoided being arrested for causing a riot!'

I added the last words out of sheer self-defence, figuring that attack is the best form of defence. I was astounded by his reply.

'Came to nothing? Nonsense, my dear fellow, it may not quite have produced the outcome I had hoped for, but the whole episode has been very productive.'

'How can you say that, Holmes, for no one attempted to steal the painting as you had expected them to. Why the best that happened was the sight of the fellow who hung around rather a lot. But he gave no key to his identity.'

Sherlock Holmes pushed his plate from him, reached for a pipe and filled it with the South African shag. His eyes twinkled as he lit it and sank back in his chair. Then he fixed me with those gimlet eyes of his and delivered his bombshell.

'Watson, the fellow could not resist signing his painting whilst alone with it in the bar. He used the paint in my art box which if you remember was beside the picture. Careful, the paint is still wet!'

His last words were produced by my sudden movement toward the painted panel.

'Upon my word, he has not exactly signed it, but he has painted a style or monogram in the lower right corner. Can you make anything of it, Holmes?'

'I have no doubt that I will be able to make something of it, Watson. In fact this is as good a time as any to make a start.'

He took up his lens and propped the painting up by the elegant means of leaning it against a pile of books and scrap albums. Then he opened the blinds to increase the daylight and peered at the tiny design. After a minute or so he handed me the lens and asked for my own opinion of it. I scrutinized it carefully. I could make out a roughly heart-shaped frame with a shape within it which one could, I suppose, consider to be rather like a cliff. I took a stab at it.

'Perhaps Clifford Love?'

'Good thinking, Watson. I can only offer Hart, spelled without an "e" as an alternative surname. But I think we can only at this stage take the painting to an expert. I feel sure that my old colleague, Sir Wilfred Greenwood, could help us.'

Holmes's colleague, Sir Wilfred, operated a gallery in London's Bond Street, where we stood in admiration of the many wonderful paintings which he had on display. He was delighted to be of service and after Holmes had introduced us he exhibited a business-like zeal that had doubtless put him at the top of his profession.

'My dear Holmes, Dr Watson, I tremble with excitement whenever I see a shrouded canvas, for one never knows what is about to be revealed. It's the thrill of a possible great discovery.'

I dared to make a pertinent remark at this point. 'It is, Sir Wilfred, painted upon a piece of artist's board rather than on canvas.'

His reaction surprised me. 'All the more exciting! Do you know I once purchased a Lautrec that had been executed on a paper table cover at the Moulin Rouge. He was not even particularly famous at that time, but I knew that it was a good investment. So please, gentlemen, unwrap your surprise package and put me out of my suspense.'

Holmes unfurled the cloth in which he had very carefully wrapped the board, on account of the wet style or signature. He placed it upon the easel toward which Sir Wilfred indicated with an artistic gesture. The noble art dealer examined the painting with growing interest.

'My dear Holmes, you have here an undoubtedly unknown work by Clifford Harty. Were you involved in my world you would know that Harty became very fashionable about ten years ago. I could have got him numerous commissions to paint portraits of the great and famous. But he would not undertake such things and preferred the more difficult path of painting his own subjects and allowing me to sell them for him. This is a typical example of his later work, but it puzzles me that it is painted upon board. It is very recent indeed as far as his signing is concerned, yet the paint in general has settled to a point that it would normally reach after two or maybe three years. In other words he has recently signed work which he did not sign at the time of execution. I wonder why?'

'It is a valuable painting then?'

'It is worth many thousands!'

'Solely on account of the brilliance of his work?'

'Only partly so. The value is also in the fact that it is an unknown work of such a popular artist who appeared to vanish from the face of the earth a few years back. Yet I do not believe him to be dead. He sold me a painting, the last I obtained from him, a few years back, and then I heard nothing more from him.'

'How did he seem in his manner?'

'Troubled, like a man with a burden to carry. By the way, I do not recognize the model in your picture. Generally he used the same two or three models. This was painted on the coast, perhaps she is a local girl?'

At this point Sir Wilfred was obviously himself requesting information from Holmes in return for information given, but this was only very gently inferred. Holmes kept faith by telling Sir Wilfred as much of the story as he could.

In other words, nothing concerning the tragic events, but giving him the story of our finding the picture and the device that Holmes had used which had resulted in the strange appearance of the signature. Greenwood realized that Holmes was holding back that information which he was not at liberty to divulge. He confined his next remarks to the bizarre ghostly signing. We described the suspicious artistic character whom we had observed, but Sir Wilfred was unimpressed by this description.

'You could be referring to Clifford, but most of my artists are bearded and roughly clad. However, he was there and he did sign it, because that is his design. I can scarcely call it a signature really.'

Upon our arrival back at Baker Street we found a surprise visitor awaiting us in the sturdy shape of Inspector George Lestrade of Scotland Yard. Lestrade was an old colleague of ours, a down-to-earth police detective of the old school, intelligent and reasonable despite his plodding nature. So often in the past had Holmes been able to add that little touch of brilliance that had given the journeyman investigator the cherry to put upon his cake. After the usual niceties of greeting Holmes, remembering these occasions, waxed ironical.

'Well, Lestrade, what can I do for you? Is there some little point that a non-professional can make that will spark the very thought that will lead to you solving a case?'

But the inspector's reply made Holmes regret his sarcasm instantly!

'No, Mr Holmes, I am simply here as a friend to warn you that your lady colleague, Miss Adler, is about to be arrested upon several charges including, the worst, for being an accessory to unlawful killing. Dr Watson and yourself will be lucky to avoid being involved too, if Inspector Cummings can dream up some charges; anything from wasting police time to concealing evidence. I know all three of you well enough to realize that none of you are implicated, but you have upset a very ill-mannered and bad-tempered individual. He could make a great deal of trouble for you, aye and for me too if he found out that I had given you this hint. But, well, you have indeed been more than helpful to me on occasion, Mr Holmes, and I regard you and the doctor as friends, if that is not presumptive of me?'

Holmes has ever been embarrassed by such words, but he handled the situation with diplomatic mastery.

'My dear fellow, your words touch me, and I have always regarded you with the utmost respect. I realize the risk you have taken in bringing me this information and I will not let you down, believe me. But now if you will excuse me I must make use of your warning and return to the south coast without delay. Watson, pack yourself an overnight bag, and I will do the same. We must be on a southbound train within the hour.'

Lestrade left us, and upon the stairs he whispered to me, 'He is looking well, Doctor. Thank heaven he is up and around again, even if he does end up in prison!'

Lestrade's last words had suddenly reminded me of just how very unwell my friend had been until little more than a week earlier. I could not now believe that only a few days had gone by since I had feared for his sanity and even for his life. The wonderful transformation seemed worth the risks that had become involved. For, yes, we had concealed evidence which we should really have passed on to the police, and Holmes was still concealing evidence in the shape of the Clifford Harty painting. Of course, when I came to think about it, everything came down to me, for had I not concealed from the authorities that knife and bloodstained dress and presented them to Holmes, the real tragedy in which we had become involved would never have been discovered. But then, I mused, I could equally blame Irene and Mycroft, who had unwittingly plunged us all into the *Mon Repos* affair.

Sherlock Holmes, however, was quite undismayed by this recent turn of events. I noticed that he carried very little luggage, but did have the carefully wrapped painting under his arm.

As we hurtled toward the south coast at almost fifty miles an hour, he said, 'Watson, we may well be in time to save Miss Adler from the unfortunate event which threatens. I may have no alternative but to provide Cummings with a distraction by putting our cards upon the table before the winning hand is complete. If I present him with the painting and the story of its signing and all that Sir Wilfred has told me, he may not go after Miss Adler. But be warned, Watson, he may still go for me. You may yet need to instruct Mrs Hudson to bake me a pie with a file inside it!'

He laughed harshly at his own humour, whilst I reminded him of my own implication in the whole affair.

Again he laughed. 'My dear fellow, no one could suspect

such a pillar of the community as yourself of being a criminal. Don't worry, I don't think either of us will break any stones.'

We reached the Jolly Smugglers to be greeted by Irene, who looked radiant as ever but with a suppressed air of excitement. She insisted on ordering dinner for us and making a point of having it put on her bill. I had read a little of *The Modern Woman*, but felt that she was taking this to an extreme.

Suddenly we were interrupted in the consumption of the gastronomic delights of a lobster straight from the estuary. Cummings arrived, with Sergeant Cooper, without any sort of a polite entrance.

'Ah, there you are! I came to arrest one of you, but now you have saved me the trouble of contacting London by returning, gentlemen. I have been to Manchester on a wild-goose chase and have been forced to consider that my suspects are nearer home.'

'The lobster is excellent, my dear inspector. Pray do partake of some. But then I am forgetting my place . . . you see we are, all of us, guests of Miss Irene Adler.'

Holmes spoke calmly and with a barb in his tongue. The inspector replied by snapping, 'Miss Adler is in danger of becoming a guest of Her Majesty, Holmes, so don't come the comedian with me. You have stuck your toe into a rockpool that does not concern you, so unless you have something sensible to tell me, please hold your silence.'

Sherlock Holmes smiled benevolently as he spoke in icy tones. 'Inspector, I indeed have some things to tell you and indeed something to show you, pertinent to your enquiries.

But first, may I ask upon what charges you mean to threaten Miss Irene Adler, who is by the way an American citizen and entitled to be treated with courtesy.'

'Mr Holmes, Miss Adler has admitted to finding a bloodstained butcher's knife and a bloodstained woman's dress in a bungalow which she had rented. Instead of bringing these items to our knowledge, she placed them in a hat box and treated this as left luggage at Victoria Station in London. She has a cock-and-bull story about dropping the ticket for this box so that Dr Watson would find it and take it to you! I went to this Mycroft Holmes for confirmation as you suggested. But whilst he was very plausible and fooled me at first, I am beginning to think that he, too, might be implicated in the crime in some way. Unless you all come up with the truth, and it reassures me, I will be forced to arrest Miss Adler, and I don't care if she is a Pomeranian!'

The inspector seemed in danger of losing control of himself, his face reddening and his hand starting to shake. But Holmes did not fall into the trap of answering his angry words with similar style.

'My dear Cummings, do please take a little wine, it will calm you. Now let me say this, in order to arrest Miss Adler I believe that you would need a more specific charge than the concealment of evidence. She may well say that she considered the course that she took was a wise one. After all, she drew my attention to the matter and in turn I drew yours to it.'

'Why did she not go straight to you rather than enact the three-act drama with the hat box?'

'Because I was extremely ill. I would probably have refused to see her, or not even been able to recognize her.'

The inspector grunted. 'A likely tale; you look well enough to me. Anyway, I could find another charge upon which to hold Miss Adler: impersonating a man in a public place for instance. I think we could find a word to cover a person who does such things!'

Holmes smiled indulgently and replied, 'Miss Adler appeared in public only as herself. She was permitted to dress in any way she might wish upon premises which she had rented. She would tell you that she was rehearsing for a modern opera in which she plays dual roles of husband and wife. I would not go down that road, Inspector, you could be made to look absurd. But why do you not put all this to one side, for I have evidence to offer and of a nature which may help you to solve the whole case.'

Cummings said nothing, but was all attention when Holmes produced the painting. Holmes and I joined, or alternated, in telling the inspector of the events that had followed our discovery of the picture, the adventure of the Chelsea public house which had resulting in the mystery signing, and the views given us by Sir Wilfred. Sergeant Cooper worked fast with his pencil and notebook.

Cummings examined the picture carefully. He was still irritated, but was at least more calm in his manner toward us. 'You should have brought this straight to me!'

'You were in Manchester.'

'If I had handled the matter, the fellow who signed it might not have got away.'

'Would you have taken the picture to Chelsea at all?'

'That is beside the point. Then you took it onto yourself to consult this expert.'

'Can you not benefit from his information?'

'Well, well, perhaps . . .'

A diversion at this point occurred when the landlord brought our suet pudding. He looked at the painting with interest and some surprise.

'Bless my soul, it's Margery Williams! I haven't set eyes on her for two or three years. What would someone be doing painting a picture of poor little Marge?'

Holmes leapt in before Cummings could startle the landlord or make him wary of speaking his mind.

'You knew her then, landlord?'

'Knew her, sir? Why she often worked in this very room as a barmaid. Good worker she was, even if she did have some funny ideas. Tried to tell people that she had been an artist's model and had been painted by famous men. Last I knew someone had, forgive me, Miss Adler, got her into trouble. I always assumed she left the district on account of that.'

As the landlord returned to his work, Holmes pushed his plate away from him with the intention of ignoring his suet pudding. I could not resist tampering with mine until he caught my eye, his gimlet orbs glowering their message for me to desist. Then he spoke as if to finalize the whole affair of the mystery of *Mon Repos*.

'Well, Inspector, I believe you have received all the evidence that any of us could give you, the landlord's bonus being as much as a surprise to me as to you. Clifford Harty used Miss Williams as his model, but neither of them spoke of this to anyone in the locality.'

I felt forced to interrupt. 'But, Holmes, I know that *Mon Repos* is on the Dolphin's Spine and not very much populated. But do you not think it likely that someone would have seen him working on this painting? It is outside and you, yourself, mentioned the lighthouse in the background giving indication of where it was painted. I am no artist but I know enough about the subject to be able to say that it would have taken several days to complete.'

Holmes nodded approvingly, to my surprise. 'An excellent observation, Watson, but have you considered the possibility that Harty might have painted the scene without his model and decided to add her to the picture at a later date?'

'No, such a thought had not occurred to me and I fail to see how you could know if such a procedure was followed.'

'Watson, I am convinced that this was so for several reasons. Observe the paint of the background. This is quite dry and any artist would tell you that it was painted more than three years ago. But now observe the paint upon the figure of the woman, it is dry, yet has a certain glossiness which it will lose within perhaps another twelve months. Aside from this, observe the shadows in the background scene, they are deep and unmistakably natural as if produced by natural sunlight. The figure in the foreground has been artificially lit; there are no deep shadows.'

He handed me his lens and I had to agree that he was right on all counts.

Cummings was as near to being impressed as I suppose

he would ever be. He enquired, 'So we have the identities of both victim and criminal. It should be easy enough to find relatives or friends of the girl. As for the artist, if he decides to disappear or change his appearance we may never get him. But what was his motive in doing what he did? Why did he not get her to a hospital? Do you consider that he might have been the father of her child and wanted the matter kept quiet?'

Holmes considered carefully before he replied. 'I doubt that, for he had money and was a bohemian who would have cared little what people thought of him. She, poor girl, may have considered that her condition had gone undetected and may have begged him not to divulge anything of it. She could have managed to get him to think that between them they could deliver the child. I suppose all of this makes you need to arrest him, Inspector, though quite what the charge might be I am not really sure. He did not mean to kill her, and when she had died he tried to save the child. He had just got in too deep to come clean and decided to bury them in the hope that they might not be discovered until such time as the whole thing would be unimportant through much passage of time.'

It was Cummings's turn to look thoughtful. Then he said, 'I could charge him with practising medicine without a licence and failing to report two deaths upon premises which he occupied.'

All of this time Irene Adler had remained quiet and almost motionless. So when she did move, and speak, she had all attention. 'Inspector, suppose a third party had been involved, would that reduce the severity of punishment should Harty be arrested?'

The inspector spoke carefully, 'That would depend upon the circumstances. If this third party, for example, alone attempted to deliver the child, I believe it would affect the severity of a sentence. Especially if he was acting more upon his own intention than that of the resident of the bungalow, Mr Harty. But we have no reason to believe that such a third party was involved.'

There was a short silence broken by Sherlock Holmes who spoke very directly and incisively to Irene, yet managing to get a note of kindness into his voice.

'My dear Miss Adler, if you know of anything which I have missed during my investigations, I feel that you should tell the inspector about it.'

She coloured slightly, then recovered her composure. 'Sherlock, my dear, I have the greatest possible admiration for you and your methods and your incredible intellect. What I have learned I merely stumbled upon and you would have discovered it yourself given time.'

Holmes smiled at her kindly and spoke more gently. 'Miss Adler, you are a highly intelligent woman as through the years I have grown to know. It would be absolutely no insult to your humble servant should you have deduced and discovered where I had missed out. I will not be offended!'

She still hesitated, to the point where you could have heard a pin drop. Then she spoke and clarified the mystery that she had first to explain. 'While you and the doctor were in London, discovering so much that has proved to be of such value, I kept my eyes and ears open. Of course, I had a few business matters to clear up locally connected with my short sojourn at *Mon Repos*. Settlement of rent and tradespeople, and so on.'

Cummings was growing impatient. 'Miss Adler, I must warn you . . .'

Sherlock Holmes rounded on him. 'Inspector Cummings, Miss Adler has something to tell us which I anticipate to be of prime importance, especially to your good self. It is to be hoped, therefore, that you will allow her to impart it at her own speed, indeed in any way she wishes to.'

Cummings grunted, but inclined his head in some kind of a grudging assent.

Irene continued. 'It so happened that on a number of occasions I used the services of a Mr Murray, who drives a brougham that has seen better days. He is, as you may know, one for a gossip. He was full of his past association with Dr Watson during the Afghanistan campaign and of his part in the doctor's rescue in the heat of battle. Actually this was no news to me because Sherlock and John had already informed me regarding Murray's sudden appearance and after so many years. But when I mentioned this to the landlord of this establishment he brought forth a variation on the story. You see, Murray had told me that he had started up as a cab driver in this area very soon after the Afghan war, using his discharge payment in order to purchase the old war-horse, Captain, and the vehicle which he had found locally for a mere song.'

I felt that I needed to bolster her story at this point.

'That is exactly what he told me. You were present, Holmes, so I feel sure you remember the conversation?'

Holmes backed me up, in turn. 'I remember the incident and the words extremely well. He also mentioned having been your medical orderly as well as having saved your life.'

Irene continued her narration. 'Well, a night or so back Murray came into this bar and insisted upon making confidences to me. Remember, he was the worse for drink. But he spoke convincingly enough of helping Dr Watson to deliver some of the tribeswomen's babies, where there were complications. He even went into details concerning one such occasion when he had helped you to perform a tracheotomy. After another tankard of ale he changed the subject somewhat, and forgetting the story of the purchase of horse and cab with his army pay he began to tell me that he had purchased these far more recently with some money that he had earned by, to quote his own words, doing a gent a turn and giving him a hand.'

There was a silence at this point that you could have cut with a knife.

It was broken by Holmes, who looked admiringly at Irene as he complimented her. 'My dear Miss Adler, you do yourself an injustice when you infer that all this information fell into your lap. Come, dear lady, I am an investigator of some experience and I realize that to extract all that information from Murray was the result of rather more than being a good listener.'

She hesitated a little. 'Well . . . well, I may have asked him the odd question. When he responded as if flattered by my interest, I certainly let him ramble on that he might tell me more.'

Holmes chuckled. 'You hardly needed him to say more, as I think the inspector will agree. If I am any judge of human nature, and I am considered to be in certain quarters, Murray will confess everything if he is handled sympathetically and offered even a hint of a light sentence.'

Inspector Cummings seemed like a man transformed. Where Holmes had failed to gain even his grudging admiration during the investigations, Irene had captured it completely.

'Miss Adler, I congratulate you on your sagacity and enterprise. On reflection, I apologize for any hint of accusation I may have made against you. I realize now that out of frustration I was clutching at straws.'

It turned out, by chance, that Murray himself appeared upon the scene shortly after, quite unaware of being suspected of anything. He made a line for us but the open smile soon disappeared when Sergeant Cooper dropped a hand upon his shoulder and made the official charge and arrest. Murray said little, but looked at me beseechingly as he was led away.

I did what I could for Murray, managing without much difficulty to engage the landlord to store Murray's carriage in his barn and give the horse the freedom of his meadow. At least my old comrade would have his business to return to. Needless to say, I spoke up for him in court and was happy to see him get the absolute minimum sentence for his part in the *Mon Repos* affair. This was only partly through my intervention, and mainly through his being able to supply information which led to the arrest of Clifford Harty. Although the artist did not himself perform the illegal operation leading to the death of his unfortunate model, it was felt that he was thought to be, as a man of education, more able to understand the serious nature of the illegal procedure. But I was rather glad that both of them would be abroad again within a couple of years.

When Miss Adler, Holmes and I had returned to London, Mycroft arranged a splendid dinner at Simpson's in the Strand for the four of us. During the meal and between the courses the brothers Holmes indulged in a lightning exchange of deductions, so fast in its delivery and exchange that there was no time for them to explain anything. Indeed it became obvious that they understood the working of each other's minds too well for any kind of *modus operandi* to be needed.

'I see, Mycroft, that you changed your mind twice concerning which cravat you should wear . . .'

'Correct, and I notice, my dear Sherlock, that you lost your right cufflink and found it again only a few minutes before leaving Baker Street.'

'At about which time you were changing your mind concerning the purchase of an evening newspaper, plumping for a magazine.'

'Must we be so elementary, my dear Sherlock? What occupation would you say is followed by the stout diner at the next table?'

'Stockbroker, but not always so, for he started out as a solicitor's clerk.'

'Don't forget his sojourn in Italy a few years back.'

'Curiously in the same province where the head waiter was born.'

'Born, yes, but not raised there. The fellow was taken from Italy to America at a very early age.'

'How about the companion of the stout man? Aside from the fact that she is a typist and lives in Maidstone.'

'She is Welsh on her father's side, with a Scottish mother.'

'Twenty-three, engaged but called it off three times.'

Twenty-two, and called it off twice. The third engagement was called off by the man involved and resulted in a breach of promise action.'

Irene touched my arm and voiced my own thoughts. 'You know, John, a hundred years ago they would have been burned as witches! How do they do it, absorbing each other's deductions at such an incredible speed?'

I chuckled as I replied, 'I don't know, but I'll wager they were insufferable as children. As it is, they could go on the halls as a sort of mind-reading duo!'

Then when the meal had been cleared away and the repartee had ceased, Mycroft rose to his feet, his glass in his hand. He proposed a toast.

'Ladies and gentlemen, dear friends, may I propose a toast to my brother in joy and gratitude that he has been reclaimed by his friends. Raise your glasses, please, in salute to the world's greatest detective, so nearly lost to that world. Sherlock Holmes!'

We all three raised our glasses and Holmes bowed his head in some sort of gratitude. Then he rose to his feet and proposed a toast in his turn.

'Dear friends, I would like to thank you for my redemption. I realize now that life is worth living and that I am still capable of being useful to my fellow man. But Mycroft, when you were kind enough to call me the world's greatest detective, you may be in error. You know, it was really Miss Adler who supplied the missing piece in the affair at *Mon Repos*. Could it be that the world is as yet ready for a great female investigator? Please raise your glasses to . . . *the* woman!'

Many more toasts were proposed and drunk, and it was a very happy evening indeed. Then, just before we were about to go our various ways, I realized, through a sea of champagne, that I had not myself proposed any toast. I rose unsteadily to my feet and then forgot what I was standing there for.

Holmes told me later that I had raised my glass and said, 'I *was* right, old Captain *was* a grey!'